D1206876

For the Strength of You

Compilation and Introduction copyright © 2005 by
Triple Crown Publications
2959 Stelzer Rd., Suite C
Columbus, Ohio 43219
www.TripleCrownPublications.com

Library of Congress Control Number: 2005927133
ISBN# 0-976234971
Cover Design/Graphics: www.MarionDesigns.com
Author: Victor L. Martin
Editor: Chloé A. Hilliard
Production: Kevin J. Calloway
Consulting: Vickie M. Stringer

First Trade Paperback Edition Printing August 2005
10 9 8 7 6 5 4 3 2

Printed in the United States of America

DEDICATIONS

I'LL LET THE SONGS SPEAK FOR MY FEELINGS

Sandra J. Martin (Mom) = B.I.G.: Sky's the Limit

Angie R. Martin (Sis) = Ja Rule and Mary J. Blige: Rainy Dayz

Dominique A. Covington (Newphew) = Slick Rick: Hey Young World

Janayia A. Martin (Niece) = Keith Murray: The Most Beautifullest Thing

Tremika M. Smith (Sis) = Mary J. Blige: My Life

Vickie Stringer (A Blessing) = G-Unit: Smile

Kontar Joyner (My Nigga) = Main Source: Looking At The Front Door

Kim A. Carroll (My Ace) = Seether and Amy Lee: Broken

Keama T. Eason (Princess) = Tribe Called Quest: Relax Yourself

My Entire Family = Lost Boyz: Dedication

T.C.P. = Lost Boyz: Get Up

Theme Song for this Novel:

B.I.G.: Unbelievable

ACKNOWLEDGEMENTS

I've been blessed again.

I'm thankful to still have my best friend/typist Kim A. Carroll, where would I be without you?

To all of my readers that supported my first two novels, *A Hood Legend & Ménagé A Way*, thank you deeply. There's no me without you. I must put a plug in for *Complex* magazine for doing the first article about me, thanks for the publicity.

On days I faced writers block, it was broken down by tuning into the Butta Team on WNCU 90.7FM, the official number one street DJs. While I'm on the radio, I gotta send love to Mary Jane at WQOK 97.5FM, thank you for your words of encouragement...now drop down and get your eagle on girl!

If anyone in Havelock, N.C. can reach my right hand man, Shaft, tell him to get at me. I owe you plenty! Karen Hamilton of New Bern, N.C., look, what you started and the masterpiece can still be yours. Yeah, I'm still on lock, but I refuse to be broken!

Keama Eason...I guess I know the meaning of a true friend, thank you for understanding me.

To everyone that calls Johnston County home, you know I had to pen one for the Dirty-Dirty.

To all my peeps: Sherwood, Decky, Varis, D.C., Patrick

III

Triple Crown Publications presents

Kent, Pig, Tremain, Casual C., Hands, Pee Wee, Markie, Ant Man, Do-Right, T.J. Williams, Vick Tug, Shawn, Fonz, Shan, Mitchell Holmes, A.K.A. Big Chubb, Michael Peacock, Von, Fish, Eddie Davis, Jerome and if I didn't plug you in on this one, forgive me.

And to all my ex's and one-nite stands…picture that! Yeah, I'm out of sight and out of mind…for now. I'll stay humble and I'll stay true. Thank you all for believing in me.

Chapter 1

Selma, North Carolina

****

Redwood Village Apartments
ATTENTION POLICE:
NO TRESSPASSING
NO LOITERING
NO SOLICITING
ANYONE SEEN IN VIOLATION OF
THESE RULES SHOULD BE
ARRESTED

Friday, July 4th weekend...

"Yo, Anshon!" Fe-Fe snorted into the crack of the back door, with snot dripping over her ashy black lips. "It's me nigga, Fe-Fe. Where you at, yo?" Anshon was pissed. His dick was hard and all he wanted to do was fuck Constance, his bad ass white chick, who laid in the bed waiting for him. "Anshon, it's me, Fe!" Fe-Fe yelled again, her lips plastered into the crack of the door.

Anshon took his 9mm off the kitchen table and placed it in the waistband of his sweat pants. He yanked the back door open and Fe-Fe stumbled inside. "My nigga," Fe-Fe grinned, with slob sliding down the side of her mouth. Anshon closed the door and Fe-Fe stood up straight. She pulled the belt of her dingy yellow raincoat tight around her tiny waist, reached in her back pocket, and snorted again, "I got some dough nigga and I ain't have to suck that much dick and shit. Look." She cupped her hands and showed him a ten dollar bill and five dollars in change. There were a few bottle caps in the mix, but after she took them out, she handed him the money. "On the real, a bitch needs a twenty spot."

"A twenty spot?" Anshon frowned, reluctantly taking her money. "You ain't suckin' my dick and shit. With all these ma'fuckin' quarters, yo' ass gotta be short."

"Look," Fe-Fe said, looking around the room. "You know I be having to give all my money to my cousin, the one who got my kids and shit. I'm good for it though, for real. Soon as my check come in next month, I'ma hit you up."

Anshon shook his head. Fe-Fe always had an excuse why her money was short. "Don't come up short no damn more!" he snapped, reaching into the carpenter pocket, on the side of his sweat pants and pulling out two vials of crack.

Fe-Fe's whole face lit up. "Boy, you know how it is. I ain't got my check yet." She took the two vials into her hand. "This is that good shit, right? That shit Jinks OD'd off of?"

"Somthin' like that," Anshon said, annoyed and wanting Fe-Fe to leave. Opening the door, he frowned at her. "Bounce 'fore my girl come down here trippin'."

"That is a bad ass white bitch you got." Fe-Fe wiped the string of snot dripping from her wet nostrils with the back of her hand and snorted what she could back into the bridge of her nose. "She damn near looks like that Brittney Spears trick. But you know I look better than that hoe, right? Humph, don't sleep." Fe-Fe snapped her fingers and twirled around. "Ain't no pussy like a black woman's pussy. Word up, you ought a come through and see about a bitch one day." Fe-Fe winked her eye and turned to walk away, "Be good Anshon," she yelled over her shoulder, happy that she had what she came for.

It had only been six months since Anshon hit the streets, after doing a two-year stint. His dough was low and every little bullshit penny counted. Locking the door behind Fe-Fe, he unballed the ten-dollar bill and counted out the change. *Fuckin' chicken*, Anshon thought while throwing the money into his pocket. "I'm so sick of this bullshit," he moaned, as he headed up the stairs to Constance. "But a nigga gotta eat."

Young Buck's "Shawtie Wanna Ride" played from behind the closed bedroom door. Anshon stroked his dick as he thought about Constance being spread eagle, dripping wet, and waiting on him. He turned the knob and opened the door. Constance was standing with her back to him, dressed in a pink Nike t-shirt, with nothing underneath, moving her head to the music, and ironing her green Department of Corrections uniform.

"What you doin'?" he asked her, lifting the shirt above her waist and pressing his hard dick into her apple bottom ass. One of the things he liked about her was that she had a sista's ass and she never tripped off no black and white shit. Her mouth wasn't on fire like some of the black chicks he fucked here and there. And Constance understood that there was a distinct difference in a nigga being broke and one on the come up. Anshon was sure that a sistah would've fronted on him a long time ago.

"You know I gotta go to work," Constance said, pressing the iron into the crease of her pants.

Anshon took two of his fingers and played in her wetness, "Let me hit it real quick."

"Why it gotta be quick?" she smiled, cutting the iron off and yanking the cord from the socket.

"Oh you want some of this dick?"

"That's what it is?" she teased.

"You tell me what it is." Anshon took his gun from his waist and placed it on the nightstand. Slowly, he started kissing the back of Constance's neck while bending her over. She placed both of her hands on the ironing board and he dropped his pants. He parted her vaginal lips with his dick. Sliding his dick in, he started pounding hard and intense strokes into her wetness.

"You better kill this pussy!" she moaned, as Anshon

took one of his hands and flicked his fingers across her clit. "Damn, this is why I started fucking with you."

"Why?" he asked.

"'Cause you know how to work that big dick." She started throwing her ass and working her pussy against his shaft.

"I was in prison when you started fuckin' me, *C.O. Connelly*," he said sarcastically, "So, what made you think that I had a big dick?" Anshon bit the inside of his cheek in an attempt to fight off the nut, he felt creeping up.

"Cause I watched you in the shower...you ain't never gun me down or beat your meat in front of me, I had to see it some how," she said.

"So you saw it and what?"

"And this..." Constance turned around toward Anshon, causing his dick to slip out. She got down on her knees and started hittin' him off with some head. Sucking her dripping juices off his dick, she took her right hand and started tickling his balls.

Anshon's neck rolled back as his nut broke lose. "Goddamn you!" he moaned grabbing a fist full of her auburn hair and pushing his dick further into her mouth. Constance grabbed both of his tight ass cheeks and swallowed his nut.

"You like that shit, don't you?" She smiled, wiping the corners of her mouth and getting off her knees.

"That's wassup," he said pulling his pants up.

She kissed him on the cheek. "You gonna spend the night?"

"Nah."

"Please." She placed her uniform in the crook of her arm.

"Stop worrying. I'll be here when you get offa work. I gotta go check on my sister, Tammy, she's been calling me to come through."

"I love you Anshon," Constance said hugging him.

"You don't love me," he smirked, squeezing her ass, "you love this dick."

****

After showering and changing into the extra set of clothes he kept at Constance's crib Anshon jumped in his black and slightly rusted, '72 Chevy convertible.

He placed his work, which consisted of an eight-ball of crack and a bundle of dope, inside his glove compartment and locked it. Anshon knew it was a dumb move to be riding with vials of crack on him, but he was hoping to run into one of the local hustlers or street runners, who were looking to push a lil' weight for the 4th of July weekend.

Slowly, he cruised down Lizzie Street, poppin' his hydraulics, and taking in the sights. It was two a.m. and Selma, North Carolina was live. Firecrackers were blazing the sky, the scent of purple haze floated in the air, and everybody who wasn't outside on their porch, was in the local shot house or the barbeque pit—which doubled as a club—gettin' their crunk on.

"Anshon! Yo! Anshon!" A tiny voice yelled from down the block.

When Anshon looked to see who it was, he saw Fe-Fe waving him down. He stopped the car and she ran over to the window. He knew right away that she was high. "Can you run me 'cross town?"

"Run you cross town? You runnin' from 5-0 or something? Don't bring me no ma'fuckin heat, Fe-Fe."

"Come on now," Fe-Fe frowned, "I wouldn't go out like that. On the strength of your sister, Tammy, if nothing else."

Knowing that Tammy was his soft spot, Anshon smiled. "Where you goin'?"

"Sumner Street," Fe-Fe smiled.

He sucked his teeth and nodded his head toward the passenger seat. "Get in."

"You ain't hittin' the block?" Fe-Fe asked closing the door.

"I'm good." Anshon glanced in his rearview mirror before pulling off.

"That stuff you got is the shit. Nigga I was so high that I thought T.D. Jakes was preachin' to me. Word up, I'm goin' to church on Sunday."

"Yo' Fe, unless you wanna be walkin' you gotta shut the fuck up."

"Oh I forgot," she said rolling her window down slightly, "You don't like to discuss this shit in the car. But check it," she licked her ashy lips, "When you gon' let me give you some ass in exchange for some play? You know I'ma dime piece."

"Fe-Fe."

"Yeah?"

"Shut up.

Fe-Fe rolled her neck; she started to get smart, but changed her mind. After all, she was the one catching the ride. "How's my homegirl, Tammy, doin'?" she asked.

"She's getting better," Anshon said, making a left onto Highway 301. "Last week she got a little feeling back in her legs."

"That's good. Tell'er I said what's up and that I hope she gets better. You know we graduated Triple S High School the same year."

"'92?"

"'91," Fe-Fe smirked, "Yo'," she laughed, taking her long slim fingers and covering her mouth, "I was the shit back in the day. Sharp as a fuckin' tack. Couldn't nobody stand me and it was all good, Tammy use to say, 'Fe, they hate you 'cuz they ain't you.' Trust me, '91 was a year I ain't gon' never forget..." Anshon nodded his head as Fe-Fe went on running her mouth. "Yeah...those were the days. Club 82, The Deadend in Kenly...Shaws Ballpark. Club Kamikaze in Raleigh." She picked her cheek and popped her lips. "Damn...I forgot that one in Wilson. Yo' I use to get my party on! Fa' sho', fa' sho'."

"Was that before or after you started suckin' that

glass dick?" Anshon laughed, turning onto the exit ramp.

Oh this nigga done lost his fuckin' mind, Fe-Fe thought. "Let me tell yo' broke hustlin' ass one thang." Fe-Fe whipped her skinny neck around, to face him. "You might think you on the come up, but you just one step away from the bus, wit' yo' broke down nickel and dime ass. You ain't pushin' no Fed weight nigga. Them misdemeanor hits you sellin' is like sugary shit, so when you start sellin' that real deal, you let me know; until then, fuck you! All up in my gettin' high business. Don't you worry about when I started gettin' on. When the fuck you gon' reach baller status?"

"Hold up Fe-Fe, slow ya roll."

"No, you slow yo' ma'fuckin' roll. If you don't like what I'm sayin' then buck, suckah ass, cross-eyed nigga! You the one creepin' on the come up, not me. Matter-fact," she said pointing to the street sign, "this is my stop right here." Anshon brought his car to a screeching halt and Fe-Fe jumped out, slamming the door behind her.

Anshon sped off, rode around the block, and came back. Fe-Fe was picking her face and smiling at a trick. As Anshon rode closer to where Fe-Fe was he noticed that the trick was Constance's father, Bob. *Ain't this*

some shit, Anshon shook his head. "Yo Fe," he called to her, "Fendisha Lloyd."

Fe-Fe looked around and spotted Anshon. "Nigga is you crazy callin' me by my government all out in the street and shit?"

"Just come here," Anshon hissed.

Fe-Fe placed her hand on her hip, "Don't you see me and my man holding a conversation right here?" she pointed to Bob's chest. "How yo' bamma ass just gon' run up on me? Would you want somebody to run up on your woman?"

"Fe-Fe," Anshon yelled, "Goddamn! Can a nigga apologize?"

"Oh," she smiled. "One minute baby," she said to Bob, "Let me go see what his ass want." The passenger window of Anshon's car was down. Fe-Fe leaned on both elbows through the window. Bob was watching her ass the whole time. "I'm listening." She rolled her eyes, her breath smelling like cigarette smoke.

"Look, I apologize for the comment I made earlier."

Fe-Fe looked at Anshon and if it wasn't for how cute he was, she would've kicked his ass. His milk chocolate skin, long, zig zag parted braids, and his nice six feet tall, prison yard build; not to mention his gold tooth with the diamond in the center, was enough to drive even a sober bitch insane. "Long as you sorry for real-for real, and you ain't tryin' to play me out, we cool."

Anshon leaned over and gave her a pound. "I don't blame you for snappin'. But if you ever call me a broke down hustler again, my size fifteen will check yo' fuckin' chin."

"Size fifteen?" she giggled, "You got my coochie tinglin'! Nigga, if you a size fifteen, I'ma rape you."

"There you go with that bullshit." He couldn't help but laugh. "Peep this though, while I was locked up or even now, you ever hear anybody talkin' about who shot my sister and why?"

"Naw, all I heard is that somebody had robbed her, shot her up, and snatched her stash. What she tell you?"

"That she was switching banks or some shit and withdrew the money to take to another bank. I don't fuckin' know. But once I find out who hurt her I swear to God, I'ma spilt their ma'fuckin' wig."

"Yeah, I feel you…" Fe-Fe said, as if Anshon's comment carried her into deep thought, "it fucks me up having to see her in a wheel chair, not walking and shit."

"Yeah me too," Anshon sighed.

Fe-Fe, looked over her shoulder at Bob, who now was pacing back and forth. "Yo' Anshon, my man. My future baby daddy," she grinned.

"Baby Daddy?" he frowned, "Don't be speaking that shit into existence. We ain't that fly."

"Look, why don't you hit a sistah up real quick. This broke ass white nigga just got paid, he ready to smash, and give up some cash. Let me get some of that work you got."

"Get the cash first," Anshon smirked, "and you got whatever you need."

Fe-Fe walked over to Bob, whispered something in his ear, returned to Anshon with the cash, and they made the exchange of two vials of crack and two bags of dope. "Well, let me go." Fe-Fe stood up and smiled, "I need to go feed Bob's creamy ass some candy. You're welcome to join us." Anson didn't respond, instead he stared at her, hit the hydraulics on his Chevy, and took off.

****

"Don't cheat nigga!" Anshon heard as he rode down Lizzie Street. The twins, Wallo and Teck, were sitting on their front porch, frying fish, grilling chicken, drinking Old English 800, and playing dominos. Except for Teck's eagle tattoo on his shoulder, there was hardly any telling them apart. Football stars in high school, they had a stocky build, stood at 5'11 and where a milk chocolate brown. Rocking gold fronts, on occasion they dressed alike. The twins were always into some kind of hustle.

Anshon beeped the horn as he passed by.

"Yo Shon'!" Teck yelled, standing up and waving his hand for Anshon to come back. Anshon peeked in his rearview mirror and saw Teck. He did a U-turn in the middle of the street, and parked in front of their house.

"What the fuck is y'all doin'?" Anshon laughed, slamming his car door. "You fryin' fish and grillin' at three o'clock in the morning?"

"Don't sleep nigga," Wallo said, getting up from the domino's table to turn the fish and chicken over, "We sellin' this shit. See that lil' spot on the corner?" he pointed to the small white house with the blue lights decorating the doorway.

"Ms. Johnnie Ray's house?" Anshon smirked, giving Teck some dap.

"Hell yeah," Wallo said. "Don't let Ms. Johnnie Ray fool you, cause she always giving out Watch Towers and shit. That lil' spot is a fuckin' shot house. Niggas is drinkin' and gambling their ass off. And we got a deal with Ms. Johnnie Ray that when ma'fuckers get hungry she sends them over here to us."

"That's wassup," Teck added. "And don't be fooled, we got more than fish and chicken. Shit, we got black eyed peas, candied yams, squash, collard greens, rice, and some smokin' ass Red Velvet cake that my baby momma, Kristi, made. And you can have all of this for $4.99, fried corn bread included."

"Sounds like a hustle to me," Anshon grinned.

"Hell, yeah," Wallo gave Anshon a pound. "A nigga ain't never been so legal in his life. But in a minute, we wanna get some of that work, you know what I'm sayin'?"

"Money talks and bullshit walks," Anshon smirked, as a line of people started to form in Teck and Wallo's yard. "Y'all lil' niggas don't like to pay. It's bad enough that half of the time I can't tell you a part, but damn if I'ma be chasing you for my ma'fuckin' paper."

"Give us a hour, for real, and we gon' get you the cash. Teck," Wallo yelled pointing to Anshon, "Fix my man some food so he can chill for a minute."

Anshon ate and finished the domino game with Teck as Wallo served the long line of people. Despite it being the wee hours of the morning people were outside as if it was the middle of the afternoon. Cars were all doubled park and Teck's radio was blasting Game and 50 Cent's "In Da Club."

"Ai'ight chief," Anshon yawned, "It's 4:30 and I need to roll."

"Hold up." Wallo held his finger up.

As Anshon went to respond, Fe-Fe, who lived in the row house next to Teck and Wallo, stepped out of her house and onto her porch. "I'ma call the ma'fuckin cops on y'all black asses if you don't turn that music the fuck down, now!"

"Suck my dick ya crackhead bitch!" a male's voice yelled.

"Yo!" Anshon yelled, feeling his waist for his .9, "Who said that?"

"I did, what of it?" The male voice stepped over from the far side of Wallo's porch and revealed himself. It was Tom-Tom, Tammy's ex-boyfriend. The

17

streets always carried a rumor that Tom-Tom was the one to who had Tammy set up.

Before Anshon could get at Tom-Tom, Teck stepped up. "Ma'fucker, what is you tryna play me crazy? Startin' shit in front of my house! Don't be tellin' her to suck ya lil' nasty ass dick. You better take that shit back home to your cripple ass mama and have her suck it!"

Tom-Tom dropped the food he was eating. As he did that, most of the people standing around started to scatter.

"What...you wanna do something, Tom-Tom?" Anshon lifted his wife beater above his waist, revealing the butt of his gun. "I been wanting to blaze yo' ass for a long fuckin' time."

Tom-Tom looked at Teck, Wallo, and Anshon who by now were all standing side by side with their hands on the butts of their .9's. Tom-Tom tapped his foot and rolled his eyes. Anshon whipped out his gun and pointed it. "Apologize nigga," he said walking toward Tom-Tom. Once he got in front of him, Anshon pressed the barrel of the gun into Tom-Tom's forehead. "I wanna shoot you so ma'fuckin bad that I can taste it." Sweat started bubbling on his nose and above his upper lip. "Do you know how it feels to see my sister broken-hearted and in a wheelchair? Do you how it feels to see her not being able to take care of her kids. You were supposed to have been her fuckin' man and have her back."

"Look I-I…" Tom-Tom stuttered.

"*Look-I*-what?!" Anshon yelled. "Shut the fuck up, I'm talking!"

"Anshon," Fe-Fe ran over and stood in front of him. Her long thick jet black and wavy hair was falling over her shoulders. For once, she didn't look high and if it wasn't for Anshon knowing that she was a crack ead, he would have thought—at least for a moment—that she was beautiful. "Please don't do it." She grabbed his arm and tried to stare in his eyes, "Please. You got too much to lose. Tom-Tom ain't shit. He ain't worth it.'"

Anshon didn't budge.

"Teck! Wallo!" Fe-Fe turned to them, "Do something!"

"If the nigga buck," Teck yelled, "pop his ass!"

"Apologize," Anshon said to Tom-Tom, breathing heavy as if he were in a trance. Tom-Tom held his mouth tight and Anshon clicked the gun.

"I ain't sayin' shit," Tom-Tom protested.

"You'se a dumb nigga!" Anshon took the butt of the gun and slapped Tom-Tom diagonally across the face with it. The skin above his right eye popped open like unballing paper. Blood ran down his face like water.

"Say, 'I'm sorry'," Anshon growled. Tom-Tom stiffened and stared Anshon down. "You tryin' to punk me?" Anshon took the butt of the gun and slammed Tom-Tom across the face again; causing Tom-Tom's body to wave like a ripple in a pond.

"I'm sorry," Tom-Tom slurred as he braced his weight against the banister.

"Oh, now you wanna be sorry? I tell you what," Anshon had a crazy look in his eyes. The blood splattered gun was now pointed at Tom-Tom's face. "The next time you tell a lady to suck yo' dick, I'ma make sure you know how to suck one first!" Before Anshon would let Tom-Tom move, he ran his pockets. Anshon took $200 and three vials of crack. He handed it to Fe-Fe. "Tell her Merry Christmas!" Anshon snarled at Tom-Tom.

Tom-Tom was shakin' so bad from the stinging pain on the side of his head that he could barely get the words out, "M-M-Merry Chr-Chr-Christmas."

"Now get the fuck outta here!" Anshon shoved and kicked him in the ass as he took off running. Then he turned to Fe-Fe, "Don't bring yo' ass outside talkin' shit no more."

"Whatever," Fe-Fe mumbled on her way back into her house.

Anshon looked at Teck and Wallo, "Yo' y'all got the money or what? I'm out." Wallo handed Anshon the money in exchange for the rest of his work. Anshon got back in his car, started his hydraulics up, and sped off. It'd been a long night and Anshon wanted to get some much needed sleep.

****

"You know what nigga," was the first thing Anshon heard in the morning, as he listened to his voicemail. It was Tammy flippin' out. At first he thought he heard wrong, until he started the message over. As he did that, Constance walked in the front door, rolling her eyes and sucking her teeth. *"If I was that white bitch you fuckin' or you needed to re-up,"* the message continued, *"I would've seen your monkey ass yesterday. All I know is that you better come over here today or I'ma handle that ma'fuckin chest."* Anshon had to laugh. He pressed seven and deleted the message. Constance stood in front of him and huffed.

"What's yo' problem?" Anshon sighed.

"You, that's what."

"What about me?" he said pulling at the waist of her pants.

"Why the hell are prison inmates telling me how you had a gun to Tom-Tom's head, runnin' his pockets and shit, all over a damn crackhead?!"

"I don't know, you tell me. Why would you be hearing that all the way in prison? Especially if you work the graveyard shift. Phones go off at eight and lights go out at nine. By the time you get there most of them niggas either playing with themselves or sleep. And by the time you leave they still in the same position. So, fuck *why*, I wanna know *who* told you that shit?"

Constance stood there and looked at Anshon, she backed away from him, causing his hands to fall from her waist, "Don't try and flip the script. You just got out of prison and trouble is the last thing you need. Tom-Tom is crazy. You know he runnin' with the Jamaican mafia and shit."

"Jamaican Mafia?" Anshon laughed, "Please, Tom-Tom is a punk ass. Period. End of discussion and for the record don't ever question me about how I handle myself in the street. Understand?"

"Whatever. And another thing," Constance sucked her teeth, "you got fiends coming to my door all times of the night. My kids be here and shit. You gon' have to chill with all that."

"You know what?" Anshon snapped his fingers, "You must have another dick you suckin' on, cause you actin' like a chick with a nigga on the side. Now if I stop doing business here, then I stop coming, period. You make the choice. I don't know what the hell is wrong with your mouth but you better catch it, before my fist does. I'm out."

"Anshon! Anshon!" Constance yelled, running to block his path as he prepared to leave. "Okay, okay. Don't leave baby." She pulled him close to her and started groping his dick. "I'm sorry. I'm flippin'. It's just that I don't want anything to happen to you, Selma is a small town, and I don't want no shit jumpin' off. Okay? You accept my apology?"

He her pushed her off of him. "Bitch please," he hissed, "I don't like your fuckin' attitude."

"Don't call me a bitch!"

"Well, stop acting like one!" Anshon pushed Constance to the side and walked out the door. "I don't need this bullshit!" Anshon hopped in his car and decided to head over to his sister's crib on the other side of Selma. *I guess I'll get cussed out a second time*, he sighed to himself.

As Anshon pulled up to the gate surrounding Tammy's house he noticed that the entrance was swung open. Instantly his heart stopped and his head started to hurt. He couldn't figure out why the gate would be open when it was controlled by a numeric code. The dew from the early morning grass splashed across the toe of his Tims. He placed his hand on the knob and noticed that the door wasn't locked. "What the fuck! Tammy! Tammy! Where you at?" Anshon's heart started pounding. He pulled the gun from the waist of his pants, leaned against the front door and peeked into the living room as best he could. From the angle where he was standing, he could see nothing. He slid across the wall, so that he could get a full view of the room. Once he got to the archway, he squatted down, took cover, and ran in there. Nothing. Immediately Tom-Tom popped in his mind, *I knew I shoulda killed that nigga*. He clicked his gun. Then he reached for the nickel plated .38 that he kept in the holster around his calf. With a .9 in one hand and a .38 in the other, Anshon was determined that if somebody had hurt his sister or were setting him up for some shit, that this morning would be do or die.

From where Anshon was standing, he could see

directly into the adjoining dinning room, where he spotted Tammy's feet balled up underneath the table. The rest of her body was hidden by the curio. Tears fell from his eyes as he rushed over to where Tammy was. Once he was next to her he bent down, and rested his guns next to his thigh, he placed her head in his lap and felt for a pulse. She was alive. "Tammy," he called softly, "Come on Big Sis, you hear me?"

She snatched her hand back. "Got yo' punk ass!" she laughed. "Teach you not to come over here when I call you."

Anshon was pissed, "You play too damn much." He mushed her on the side of the head. "I should leave yo' ass right there. Where is your wheelchair?"

"I ain't using that shit! Hand me my walker from the corner over there."

Anshon put his guns away. He helped Tammy off the floor and handed her the walker. "Why would you play like that?" His heart still hadn't returned to its normal beat. "I almost shot this ma'fucker up."

"No you wasn't," she smirked, pushing her walker toward the marble dinning room table, "Yo' ass was fenin' a cry. Why they kill my sister? Boo-hoo-hoo."

"Oh that's funny to you?" Anshon helped Tammy

take a step, so that she could sit down. "What the fuck?" he rolled his eyes.

"Oh please, that shit was funny. But what I'm about to tell you is not funny. I got a call from Fe-Fe. She told me that you put a gun to Tom-Tom's head and shit."

"It was behind her ass."

"No it wasn't." Tammy frowned at him. "You did that shit because he left me. You can't fight my battles Anshon, I've been hustling a lot longer than you. And you can't mend my broken heart. Fuck that nigga. Why would you even bust a sweat over his ass?"

"Tammy, I swear I can't stand him. I just can't. I just wanna murk his ass. I know he shot you. I know he did."

"Anshon, drop that shit, for real and listen to what I want to tell you. I'm done with the game."

"What?" Anshon twisted his face.

"I'm done with the hustle. There's nothing left for me to prove. I've got some loot in the bank, my house is paid for, I have my Mercedes truck. I'm done."

"That's only half of what we can get together." Anshon sighed, "I know I've only been home for a minute and so far I've only been nickel'n and dime'n it. But come on. We can push some fuckin' weight, get Selma on lock and serve all these niggas."

"I'm tired of that. I been shot up, robbed, can't take care of my kids, and I constantly have to watch my back. The only thing left is for the Feds to run up on me. And from what I can see, ain't none of this shit worth it." Anshon sat silently. Tammy continued, "Look, what I want is for us to move to Miami. While you were locked up, I brought a little spot down there. We could move there and have a new start."

"Yo' you trippin'." Anshon got up from the table and started to pace. "Big Sis, all that you talkin' is beautiful but I need to make a few more runs and then I'll be straight. I can't kept depending on you to take care of me. Just let me in, Tammy. Tell me the connect. I know you never wanted me that deep in the game, but you gotta put me on. I promise another year and then I'm done."

Tammy shook her head no. "Don't let the game be your demise, Anshon. Please don't."

"It won't, just put me on," he begged.

"I can't do that Anshon."

Anshon walked over to the table and slammed his fist into it, "What the fuck Tammy! Why not? Don't you see how hard it is for me? You of all people should know that I don't have shit. Nobody said anything to you when you hooked up with Tom-Tom and y'all started lockin' shit down!"

"That was different, I had to take care of you!"

"You ain't take care of me, you took care of you!"

"Anshon!" Tammy yelled, "I should slap the shit out of you!" Tammy couldn't believe what she was hearing. Anshon didn't know the half of what she went through. All he ever saw was the gully, thugged out shit. The glitz, the street glamour, and the ghetto richness. So what, he'd been in prison for two years, as far as Anshon was concerned, doing time was all a part of the hustle. Somehow being behind bars made him just that much more thorough, or so he thought. In his mind it meant that, he could rock with the best of 'em. And this is what scared Tammy to death. "Don't you wanna be more than a street nigga?" Tammy asked him. "What about your football scholarship? Remember, the one you *lost* because of the streets?"

"I didn't loose that because of the streets." He looked at her like she was crazy. "I lost it because I did a bid for you. Hell, that wasn't my shit. That was your's. I took the weight because you had kids. It was my first offense and it wasn't that much shit, I was suppose to get probation remember? But instead, I got two years upstate. And what you get?" he looked around the dining room, "You got paid."

"Nigga, do you know what I did for you?" Tammy stood on her feet as best she could, "I took care of yo' black ass when Mommy died. We didn't have shit, not even a pot to piss in and a cracked window to throw it out of, and you got the nerve to talk shit to me? Our damn daddy didn't even give a fuck about us. Shit, I wasn't much older than you! But I did the best I could with what I had. I'm the one who busted my ass off a two dollar waitress' salary to take care of you. I wasn't your mother, I was your sister!" Tammy broke down and started crying. "Trifflin' ass, ungrateful nigga!"

She was only eighteen when their mother died. Anshon was twelve. Their father had remarried and wanted nothing to do with them, forcing Tammy to take care of Anshon on her own. She started as a waitress at the Waffle House and although what she made wasn't much, it was just enough to help her make ends meet. Plus, the customers loved her and those who knew her situation always gave her good tips.

Tom-Tom, was new in town and had just moved to Selma from Raleigh. From his gear, alone, everyone could tell he was a drug dealin' street nigga. Every night Tom-Tom ate dinner at the Waffle House and he always made sure to sit in Tammy's station. His pockets were laced so he was sure to always compensate Tammy for her service.

After a while of waiting on him, Tammy started checkin' for him a little bit, but knowing that he sold drugs, she knew she couldn't be bothered with him.

"Wassup shawtie?" Tom-Tom greeted Tammy as he sat down at the counter.

"May I take your order?" Tammy sucked her teeth.

Tom-Tom smiled, *Oh, she got an attitude.* "If I give you my order can you handle it?"

"Depends if we got it."

"Well look, how about you and me tonight at seven. I come by and pick you up and we go out."

"Boy is you crazy?" she flipped, "Hell naw! I know what's up with you and I ain't goin' out with no street runnin' drug nigga."

"Whoool, slow it the fuck down. You don't know me. I was trying to kick it to you because I thought you were kinda fly, that's it. Don't get it fucked up, you ain't all that. Better take that shit down."

"Well..."

"Well nothing, this was a bad idea." Tom-Tom got off the stool he was sitting on and left.

It was a week before he came back. When he walked in the door, he walked in with three of his partners. He looked at Tammy, cut his eyes, and walked the other way.

"Damn, Javette," Tammy said to one of the other waitresses, "He's going to your station. I really want to apologize for the way I tripped the other night. Please let me have that table. I'll give you the tip, whatever it is."

"Shitttt, hell yeah then," Javette agreed. "Them drug niggas be wantin' too much anyway."

Tammy walked over to Tom-Tom's table. "Hello. My name is Tammy, may I take your order?"

"Grits, eggs, and steak." Tom-Tom said not once looking up at her. "Give everybody else what they want. That is, if you can handle that. Last thing we need is a hoe trippin' and shit," he chuckled and glanced at his partners.

"First of all," Tammy snapped, "I ain't a hoe, hoe. And second of all, I apologize for trippin' on you the other night. I was wrong and I'm woman enough to admit that."

Tom-Tom laughed, "Ai'ight lil' mama, I'ma let it go, cuz I like how feisty you are. So what about tonight, when you get off?"

"Tomorrow, at seven."

"Bet, tomorrow."

After that, Tammy and Tom-Tom saw each other everyday. She loved him and without meaning to, he began to love her, which is why it took him a little over a year for him to ask her to transport for him. At first Tammy told him no, but as time went on, the harder it was to make ends meet. So eventually Tammy took Tom-Tom up on his offer and began running the drug line from Selma to D.C. and back again. During the next couple of years, they were a team and their reputation preceded them all along the eastern seaboard.

During one of her runs to D.C., Tammy came back and Tom-Tom was in jail. He'd been caught with an unregistered fire arm and because this wasn't his first offense, the judge gave him five years hard labor; leaving Tammy to run the show. And she did well for a while. Shit was going off without a hitch, until the night that she and Anshon were stopped along side of Highway 301.

Anshon had just turned 18 when he and Tammy were pulled over by the police in Raleigh. The police ran the plates and Tammy's car came back with over a hundred parking tickets, causing the police to have to seize the car.

Anshon became nervous because he knew what Tammy had tucked beneath the seats. He knew Tammy could never go to prison, because she now had two little mouths to feed. Anshon's niece and nephew were all he could think about. He couldn't see them suffer without a mother the way he did. So, he grabbed the shit and jumped out the ride with over 200 grams of coke. The police caught him only minutes later.

Tammy hired the best lawyer she could, but the best deal they got Anshon was a two-year bid. Tammy always felt guilty about her brother's situation To the best of her ability, she repped for her two niggas on lock down—Tom-Tom and Anshon. Tammy played the game as best she could. And it was all gravy until she went to the Redwood Village apartments seven months ago to collect her dough and was robbed for $287,000. She was left in the middle of the parking lot with six bullets burning in her back.

Tammy stood up straight but she could feel her knees getting weak. For a moment Anshon forgot about her not wanting to let him deeper into the game, he just couldn't believe that she was standing on her own...and for so long. "Walk," he said, almost in a whisper, "You can do it." As soon as he said that, her knees gave way and she fell to the floor. "Tammy!" Anshon said in a panic, holding his hand out to help her up.

"I don't need your help!" she pushed his hand away. Sitting up she grabbed the edge of the table and pulled herself up into the chair. Tammy looked at Anshon and tears ran from her eyes. She could see his life flash before her, and if witnessing her crippled life without her children wasn't enough for him, then she needed to give Anshon exactly what he wanted...the game.

"I'll set up the first run," Tammy swallowed hard, "Introduce you to the connect, let him make the choice of whether he wants to work with you or not, and then I'm out. Understand?"

"Yes." Anshon was trying not to smile, but he couldn't help it.

"But first, I have to share some things with you about the game."

"What?"

"If you would shut up."

"My fault," he smiled.

Tammy couldn't stand it when Anshon smiled, because his dimples would light up his face and when that happened she couldn't stay mad at him long.

"Anshon," she said, reaching for his hand, "Listen closely, I want you to know that the higher you are and the more you serving, the worst niggas get. Niggas that you ain't never seen or knew about come for your throat. Two of the most important things I want you to know are: One, you can protect yourself from your enemies, but you need God to shield you from your friends. It's always the ones you least expect. And two, keep your come up on the low. Don't buy a whole buncha new shit, keep that Chevy and ride that ma'-fucker to the ground. Don't trick your money away. Keep the white bitch suckin' ya dick. Don't give no credit, and don't shit where you sleep."

"That's more than two Tammy."

"Shut up," she laughed. "I'm just telling you. This is how you run the game, quietly. Trust me, it'll keep you alive."

Triple Crown Publications presents

Chapter 2

Six months later…

"Constance!" Teck yelled into the phone, sitting on his front porch, watching Anshon ride by, with the music from Anshon's brand new and minted '77 Chevy, leaving an echo behind. Instantly Teck became pissed, "What the fuck you mean, you don't know where that nigga keeping his stash! He floating around with a mouth fulla ice and platinum and a brand new fuckin' Chevy, plus I hear he just brought a brand new double wide, tucked away in the country somewhere. Now tell me what the fuck is goin' on! I already told my brother not to fuck wit' yo' crazy ass!"

"Don't worry about me and Wallo," she snapped ready to hang up on him. She was sick of Teck calling and harassing her. "Plus, I already told you that I don't know where his stash is. And furthermore I'm at work and I don't have time for this bullshit! Not to mention, Anshon don't be staying with me like he use to."

"I tell you what," Teck said, as he noticed Fe-Fe crossing the street, "if you don't find out about the dough, I'ma slit your throat." he hung up.

"Yo Fe," he called to her from across the street, "Where you goin'?"

She looked at him and rolled her eyes, "I'm goin' to Doughnut's."

"That fat fuck," Teck laughed. Doughnut was a local weed hustler, who ate all his money away.

I know this nigga ain't fuckin' Fe-Fe, Teck thought, *Unless he done stepped his game up and selling more than weed.* "Wallo," Teck yelled to his brother who was in the house, watching Sports Center, "Come on, let's go see what the fuck Doughnut's up to. Cause if the nigga got some cash, we gotta make plans to snatch it."

Wallo walked out of the house and onto the porch, dressed in a baggy pair of jeans, a thick gray hoddy, and some Tims. "How did *you* know I was going over to Doughnut's?'

Teck looked at his brother like he was crazy. "What

are you talking about? I'm the one who told you let's go to Doughnut's."

"Oh," Wallo sucked his teeth, "I'm going over to Doughnut's, now. This nigga got a trick over there. We 'bout to run a serious fuckin' train." He grabbed his dick, "And I swear I can't wait to fuck this freaky bitch. Word up, I know this shawtie gonna be all the way live!"

Before Teck could comment, Anshon pulled up. Teck bit the inside of his jaw as he noticed Tammy sitting in the front seat. *Damn she looks good*, he thought.

"What up dawg?" Teck said to Anshon, walking toward the car.

"You nigga," Anshon grinned, showing his brand new platinum teeth.

"Oh a nigga got new fronts," Wallo laughed pointing to Anshon's mouth, walking toward the car. When he stood next to the passenger side of the car, he leaned in and gave Tammy a kiss on the cheek. Then he said to Anshon, "Yo' I'm on my way to Doughnut's. He got a lil' jump off 'bout to blaze the spot."

"Y'all still into that shit?" Anshon frowned.

"Don't sleep nigga," Teck shook his head, "You don't run a train everyday."

"A train?" Tammy curled her upper lip.

"That ain't nothin' you gotta worry about lil' mama," Teck said, staring at Tammy. She looked so pretty in her white fox with the matching headband that instantly his dick was hard. The mid February cold seemed to fit Tammy quite well. And despite her being crippled, Teck wanted to push up on her.

Tammy could feel Teck's vibe but instead of her being at ease, that this fine ass, tall chocolate cutie was trying to kick it to her, she cringed. The stare in his dark brown eyes, scared the hell outta her. And she hadn't felt such an intense feeling of fright since she was gunned down and left for dead.

Closing her eyes, Tammy began to flashback to the day she was shot. She could see herself laying in a pool of her own blood, drowning, as the shooter, on his knees bent over and whispered in a raspy voice, *"I'm sorry."* Then he kissed her on her forehead as she laid almost lifeless. As he went to turn his back, Tammy mustered up enough strength to pull at the hem of his black tee shirt. He had a ski mask on and she desperately wanted to pull him to the ground so that she could see his face. But all she could managed to do was rip the collar of his shirt, causing the neck to stretch out of shape, revealing a tattoo of a bald eagle. A tattoo that she felt would be etched in her mind forever.

"I'm ready to go Anshon," Tammy said, shaking herself from her flash back as she opened her eyes.

He looked at her perplexed, "I thought you wanted to talk to Teck about locking down this block for us."

"Naw, maybe later. My head is starting to hurt."

Feeling uneasy, Teck stepped back from the car. "Holla at me later, Anshon. Ai'ight?"

"Yeah," Anshon said, slightly embarrassed at his sister's behavior, "I'll holla in about an hour." They pulled off.

"What was that about?" Anshon said, as they turned the corner.

"Nothing," Tammy snapped. "It's just time for me to move to Miami."

"Naw, don't give me that bullshit. You had something on your mind, spill it."

Tammy took a deep breath. "Looking at Teck made me think about when I was shot."

"How?"

"His stare," she said looking out the window and nervously playing with her hands. "Something about Teck's eyes, reminded me of the guy who shot me. Then I started having flashbacks of the eagle tattoo on his shoulder."

"Whose shoulder? Teck?"

"No," Tammy's bottom lip started to shake, "the shooter."

Anshon was confused. "How did you see the shooter's shoulder? I thought you played dead? "

"I did, but before I played dead, I yanked the hem of his shirt, revealing his tattoo, but when he turned around and stared at me, through the eyes of his ski mask. I swore, Anshon," she said wiping her falling tears, "that I would never forget that glare he had. The same glare that Teck had a minute ago."

"But Tammy how could you see all that and play dead?"

"Because after I saw the tattoo, I dropped my hand, closed my eyes, and let the blood that kept dripping down my throat, slide out the corners of my mouth."

Anshon slammed on brakes, as he almost hit the

car in front of him. He was trying to shake the visual Tammy had just laid on him. The veins in his neck felt like they wanted to explode. "I swear to God, Tammy!" Anshon yelled coming to a screeching halt and banging on the steering wheel. "If and when I find that nigga, I'ma murk his ass, execution style and that's on my word."

Tears rolled down Tammy's face, because she knew there was nothing she could say to change the way Anshon felt...and something deep inside of her didn't want to.

"But Tammy," Anshon said, "You shouldn't be scared of Teck. Teck and Wallo is damn near family."

"Family?" Tammy snapped, "When you beatin' this street, servin' these niggas, and goin' hard for that cake, it ain't no ma'fuckin family."

"Come on Tammy, *my brother's keeper-*"

"Yeah my brother's keeper, got his ass shot, trying to set up his own block."

"Yo, that's cold B."

"Yeah, and so is these streets."

****

Teck was still feeling uneasy about the way Tammy reacted to him but he tried to shake it. He twisted his lips and thought about Doughnut and Wallo. "Let me see," Teck laughed to himself, while crossing the street, "If Wallo's ass found out that Fe-Fe is the jump off."

"Wassup Teck?" Doughnut said breathing heavily as he opened the door. Doughnut's house smelled like a bad flavor of ass. "Goddamn y'all some nasty niggas," Teck said, holding his nose and watching Wallo come out of Doughnut's bedroom with his legs shaking.

"That bitch is bad," Wallo said, wiping his forehead.

"Where the hoe at?" Teck asked lighting up a purple haze big head.

"In the bathroom takin' a shower." Wallo grabbed his dick.

"Who is it?" Teck asked, waiting to hear Fe-Fe's name so that he could fall out laughing.

"Does it matter?" Doughnut frowned, "'Long as she lay and let us spray, it's all good." Doughnut sat down on the couch and switched from BET to a porno flick.

Wallo dimmed the lights and sat on the couch next to him. He reached over the arm of the couch before putting his feet on the coffee table and handed his brother two condoms, "Make good use of 'em." No sooner, than he said that did Fe-Fe step out of the bathroom, rocking a navy blue negligee with fake Fendi F's scribbled all over. The garter belt was clean, but it had two big holes in it. She looked at Teck and smiled. Her mouth lit up with two front gold teeth. Teck had to do a double take. From the neck up, Fe-Fe was a winner…and from the looks of it, if her negligee was in better condition, her body would also be a banger. She walked in front of the TV and placed her leg on the coffee table, revealing her nicely trimmed and bikini waxed pussy. Teck couldn't believe it.

"Ready for another round boys?" she winked at Teck, "Wassup with you?"

"You better go 'head." Wallo urged his brother, "Don't let the crack-head look fool you. That's just her style right now, but word up, she got some bomb ass pussy!"

Teck grabbed Fe-Fe by the arm, "You better not tell nobody but Gawd!" Teck walked in Doughnut's bedroom with Fe-Fe and frowned up his nose. Doughnut's room smelled like infected ass. Teck opened the window and motioned for Fe-Fe to sit down on the bed.

"What you want some head?" she asked. "I don't know what them niggas told you, but this pussy right here," she pointed between her legs, "Ain't a free fuck. Don't get it twisted."

"You think I want some pussy from you after you done let them two lil' niggas run up in you? Oh hell no."

"Then why you got me back here?" she frowned.

"Because I always wanted to ask you something. Why do you get high?"

"What the hell kinda question is that?" Fe-Fe rolled her eyes and placed her hands on her hip, "What the fuck you sell drugs for?"

"Sell drugs? Please that ain't even my main hustle."

"Then what's your hustle?"

"Fe-Fe," Teck smiled, "I asked you the question first."

"I can't believe I'ma answer this," she smirked, "Back in the day I use to run with Tammy and Tom-Tom. Drugs were everywhere and I wanted to try 'em. I was already a weed head but I wanted to see what crack was like and dope too. So I tried 'em."

"And that's it?" Teck frowned, "That's how you became a fiend?"

"Naw," Fe-Fe held her head down, "It started out two or three days a week and then it grew to everyday."

"You got any kids, Fe-Fe?" Teck asked sitting on the bed next to her.

"I got twin boys." Tears were starting to roll down her cheeks.

"Who's there daddy?"

"Nigga you getting' a little fuckin' personal, now. I ain't never had no nigga who wanted his dick sucked to ask me about my kids and their daddy."

"I don't want my dick sucked," Teck stroked her hair, "And I ain't just any ole nigga."

She held her mouth tight. "Their daddy is whatever nigga had the dough to get me my next hit."

"Damn," Teck said disgusted.

"See, I knew I shouldn't have told you my business."

"Naw, its cool. I'm good. Where your kids at now?"

"My cousin. She keepin' 'em until I get my act together."

"How long she had 'em?"

"For five years."

"Don't you want your kids back?"

"Ugly as I am?" she snapped, "I don't want my kids seeing me."

"Ugly?" That caught Teck off guard.

"Yeah nigga, ugly. Nobody ever told me I was beautiful. That shit always hurt me, and when I was high I realized that I could chase the pain away."

"I wonder if that's why my mom got high?" Teck said, more to himself then to Fe-Fe.

"People get high for different reasons," Fe-Fe said with tears filling her eyes. "Some reasons they can talk about and some reasons they can't. You think I like being a junkie. I just can't help it."

"I would help you," Teck said, rubbing his hand across her cheek.

"Yeah right." She twisted her lips.

"I would. But you have to want to stop getting high."

"I do."

"Well, I'll take you to the clinic tomorrow."

"Tomorrow?" Fe-Fe frowned, "Slow it down niggah. I got to get my hit on for at least two more days then we can talk about gettin' clean."

Teck looked at Fe-Fe and shook his head.

****

Anshon was decked from head to toe. He stood in front of the full-length mirror inside his walk-in closet and grinned at his reflection. This was the happiest he'd been in a long time. Tammy had hooked him up with the connect, he was gettin' paid, and servin' half of Selma and some of Raleigh while doing it. He remembered quite well that Tammy instructed him to be quiet on the come up, but some things he just couldn't resist like his minted '77 pearlized blue Chevy with 22-inch chrome Giovanni's, and a white rag top was one of 'em along with his custom designed, bricked in double wide trailer, tucked away in the country. This was the fuckin' life.

He bent down, while looking in the mirror and tied his all white Air Force Ones. He stood up straight and picked off a piece of lint from his winter white hoody. His blue Ecko jeans were perfect. He slipped on his army fatigue jacket and green Vietnam cap. His long braids hung under the cap and rested on his shoulders. And his thick Gucci link platinum chain, set it all off. Anshon couldn't help but smile, it was obvious that he was the shit.

Taking one last look at himself, he was ready to go to the pool hall and get his party on. The pool hall, was more than just a place to shoot some eight balls. It doubled as a small club, located right outside of Selma, and played Crunk music and catered to big ballers. So of course, Anshon had to be in the place. Silently approving his appearance, he reached for his car keys. As he placed them in his pocket, his cell phone rang.

"Yeah," he said, holding the phone to his ear and walking out the door.

"Yo Shon, whut up Dawg?" It was Teck.

"Nuthin', bout to roll through the pool hall. Yo' I'm sorry about earlier, with my sister. The memory of her getting shot still fucks with her."

"It's all good. I can understand," Teck said. "Why don't you come by and pick us up? Or will the twins be cock blockin'?"

"Nah, where y'all at?" Anshon asked.

"Doughnut's," Teck replied.

"Y'all still fuckin' with his nasty and crazy ass. Yo'," Anshon laughed, getting into his car and starting the engine up, "I hear his baby mama is a straight freak. He started runnin' trains on her and this bitch is turned the fuck out. My sister told me that she be hanging out in the pool hall, sucking niggas dicks and shit."

"Get the fuck outta here!" Teck laughed.

"Word," Anshon cracked up. "Ai'ight yo' I'm bout to come through, be outside." Before Anshon pulled out his yard, he called his sister, "Hey Big Sis, just calling to check on you."

"I'm good." Tammy smiled, "Just typing."

"On what?"

"Why?"

"Just tell me," Anshon pressed.

"Well since you wanna beg," she giggled. "I'm writing a book."

Anshon fell out laughing.

"See that's why I ain't wanna tell yo' dumb ass!" Tammy's feelings were hurt. "Y'all some hatin' asses."

"Whooool, slow down, Big Sis."

"No, you slow the fuck down." Tammy had a serious attitude. "This ain't a joke to me."

"I'm sorry," Anshon said, "I'm stupid sometimes, you know that. What's your book called?"

"Forget it. Don't try and get on my good side now."

"Look," Anshon sighed, "For real-for real, I'm really sorry. I wanna know the name of it."

"Okay, but you have to promise not to laugh?"

"I swear I won't."

"Hood Legend, that's the title."

"Oh word? That's tight as hell. For real. Keep it up Big Sis. You know it's all good."

"Thanks Anshon."

"Love ya girl." He hung up. Before he pulled off he slid in Lil' Jon's CD and turned the volume all the way up.

Anshon didn't live as far as everybody thought. No one but Tammy knew the exact spot of his crib and he wanted to keep it that way. It only took him five minutes to get to Doughnut's. Teck was outside on Doughnut's porch smoking a cigarette.

"Come on!" Teck yelled as Anshon pulled up. A second later, Wallo and Doughnut stepped out of the house.

Oh hell no, Anshon thought, *I never said that Doughnut's nasty ass could ride with me. Fuck that. Plus I know this nigga pockets ain't clean, he always got some shit on him.*

"Teck," Anshon yelled and motioned for him to come around to the driver's window. Teck walked around, "What the fuck? You said you and Wallo, not Doughnut. I don't want him in my ride. His ass is crazy and he always got weed and shit on him. And you know every since the pool hall started poppin' Selma's finest be stoppin' niggas all the time."

"Your point?" Teck frowned.

"My point is that his fat ass ain't riding in here."

"Come on Shon. It's all good. He been going through some hard times. He and his baby moms broke up. She got another dude that she be flawtin' right in Doughnut's face. He need to hang out with the boys for a lil' while. I'll make sure he's clean."

Anshon stared at Teck and then he gave him a pound to let him know it was all good. "Speak to his ass, first." Anshon said, shaking his head in disbelief that he was even in agreement.

Teck walked back onto Doughnut's porch, where Wallo and Doughnut were standing. "Yo'," Teck said low enough so Anshon couldn't hear him. "This nigga actin' a little retarded, ignore his ass. Y'all ready to roll?"

"Hell yeah."

They all piled in Anshon's car and took off.

"Yo, turn that shit up, Shon!" Teck said reaching for the sound system.

"Nigga is ya crazy?" Anshon laughed, "You don't never touch the radio in a black man's ride." The entire car cracked up.

As Anshon turned into the pool hall's parking lot, Lexie, Doughnut's baby's mother, watched him, ride pass her with Doughnut, Wallo, and Teck in the car. She loved to torture Doughnut and being that she was his daughter's mom that always made him assessable. Doughnut loved Lexie but he made the mistake of bringing the freak out of her, causing her to become a gold diggin' nymphomaniac.

Lexie stepped out of a tinted mid-night black Acura 3.5 RL, with red Daisy Duke leather shorts on, a long and tailor fitted red leather jacket, that fell mid-calf, red leather Go-Go boots, a red leather corset underneath the jacket, and box braids, braided with red hair that hung down her back. On her arm was Von, a ballin' nigga from Raleigh, who claimed to have half of ATL locked down.

Anshon circled the parking lot and ended up parking next to Von's Acura, where Lexie stood with Von arm and arm, preparing to make an entrance into the club.

Doughnut felt a lump rising in his throat. As he passed by Lexie, he didn't say anything but he made sure to bump Von as he passed him. Then he turned around, stared Von up and down, and gave him a look that dared him to say something.

The pool hall was packed and everybody who was somebody from Raleigh, Smithfield, and Selma were in the house. Anshon brought a Colt .45 at the bar as the twins headed for the pool tables. The music was thumpin' with Biggie's "Kick In The Door." Lexie was parading around on Von's arms and Doughnut was watching them as they continued to pass by him. He sipped his beer and leaned against the bar.

Anshon sat with his back to the bar, nodded his head to the beat and was rapping along with the song as Von came up to the bar with Lexie. Anshon glanced at Lexie and she winked her eye at him, as she and

Von ordered two bottles of beer. Anshon twisted his lips but he had to admit that, underneath all that red, she had it going on. Von looked at Anshon. "Word is," he said sipping on his drink, "That you the man I need to be speaking to."

"Is that so?" Anshon smirked.

"That's what the streets is saying," Von assured him. "Maybe one of these days I can come through and see about you?"

"Maybe," Anshon said noticing a lil' shawtie walking pass him. She was 5'5, smooth caramel complexion with full and soft looking lips that were coated with clear MAC lipglass. Her waist was small with hips that flared out and fitted her thick thighs.

Instantly, Anshon's dick was hard and he totally tuned Von out. It couldn't be denied that shawtie was boom bangin'. She had on tight jeans with Baby Phat in block letters written in pink, going straight across her ass. Not since Anshon was fuckin' with Constance had he seen such a perfect ass. Without thinking, Anshon grabbed his dick.

Destiny Child's "Souljah" started playing and everybody in the place started moving to the beat. Anshon licked his lips as shawtie started throwing her ass and dancing in the spot were she was standing.

Anshon picked up his beer and started walking toward the dance floor, leaving Doughnut standing next to Lexie and Von.

"You know if I was your man," Anshon said, pressing his dick into shawtie's ass, "I wouldn't let you out of the house, looking like this."

She threw her ass deeper into his crotch. Anshon felt like his hard on was a ticking time bomb.

"Looking like what?" she asked, still pressing her ass into his shaft.

"Like a dime."

"Oh no you didn't insult me?" she turned around toward him, her mouth twisted.

"Goddamn," he said, "untwist your mouth." Anshon took both of his hands and pushed the micro-braids that fell over her shoulders, behind her ears, revealing her name plated, gold-hoop earrings. "Damn you look good."

"For your information," she smirked looking him up and down, "I'm not a dime, I'ma twenty spot, so get yo' shit *untwisted*. And furthermore you don't know me well enough to be puttin' yo' dick against my ass."

"Not yet. I'm Anshon. Tell me your name shawtie?"

57

"Well it ain't shawtie."

Anshon laughed, "Yo', why you trippin'?"

"Ai'ight. I'ma stop buggin', my name is Monica."

"How you doin' Monica? Fine I'm sure."

"Boy please."

Anshon laughed, "Would you like something to drink?"

"Yeah. I want a Red Bull."

When she said that it reminded him of Doughnut being left at the bar with Lexie and her new man. *Where did that nigga go?* Anshon thought, while he ordered Monica's drink.

As soon as Monica took her drink into her hand, gun shots started to pop. Anshon grabbed Monica and took cover, everybody in the club hit the floor.

"Everybody put they ma'fuckin' hands up!"

When Anshon looked up, he saw three men, dressed in all black with ski masks on and Tommy guns in their hands. Oh shit, Anshon, thought, *these niggas ain't playin'. They really holdin' us up!* Just then, he heard a hissing sound. When he turned in the direction of the sound, he saw Wallo crouched down in the corner.

"Everybody stand up and shut up!" the men yelled pointing their guns.

Everyone stood up.

"Run them fuckin' pockets!" One of the other mask men yelled toward Anshon. From the sound of his voice, Anshon knew it was Tom-Tom. *Damn I shoulda killed this nigga*, he thought.

Tom-Tom looked Anshon in the face and leaned forward while running his pockets, "You should've killed me nigga."

"Don't worry," Anshon said, tight-lipped, "I will."

"What the fuck is going on?" One of the mask men yelled. "Get that nigga cash and be out!"

Tom-Tom grabbed Anshon's cash, which was only eight hundred dollars, and moved on. Everybody in the club had to empty their pockets. The men collected, money, jewelry, and even some guns. As one of them walked by, Anshon got a good look at his shape and he knew it was Doughnut. *What the fuck?* He looked toward Wallo. *"That's Doughnut,"* he mouthed.

Wallo didn't answer him, instead he nodded toward the mask men who were walking backwards out the door. Doughnut was the last man to walk out.

As Doughnut walked pass Lexie he grabbed her around the neck and pulled her with him. She started screaming. Von stood there paralyzed.

As if things had been moving in slow motion, suddenly all hell broke lose and the people started stampeding out of the club. Anshon held Monica close, picked her up and ran with her. When he got outside, he noticed Teck and Wallo running in front of him.

"Doughnut!" Anshon yelled in a panic, "That was that fat motherfucker." Anshon unlocked and snatched the door open to the car, throwing Monica inside. Teck and Wallo jumped in the back seat. As they went to take off out of the parking lot they saw Doughnut standing in front of them, holding Lexie by the neck with the gun pointed toward her head, the ski mask no longer covering his face.

"I can't believe that you did this to me," Doughnut cried, to Lexie, "As much as I loved you. We got a baby together, what did I do, tell me!" Doughnut positioned his finger on the trigger.

"Oh shit!" Wallo yelled, out the window. "Doughnut, don't, don't do it!" Anshon was trying his best to get away, but everybody was trying to come out of the parking lot at one time, creating massive chaos. Anshon could hear and smell his back tires burning rubber. Then suddenly his car shot forward, causing him to slam on the brakes. Everybody fell forward and the car behind him almost ran into the back of him.

Looking in the rearview mirror Anshon could still see Doughnut holding the gun to Lexie's head and seemed to be in a blind rage. Police sirens were blaring as they surrounded the crowd. One of them spotted Doughnut and yelled through the bullhorn, "Take cover!"

Doughnut pressed the barrel deeper into the side of Lexie's head. "Say goodnight," he slowly eased the trigger back. As he did that shots rang out from everywhere.

Anshon, Monica, and the twins ducked down in the car. It was at least 15 minutes before they looked back up again and when they did, Doughnut and Lexie were both dead.

No one said a word on the ride back home, not even Monica who'd just realized that she was riding home with a stranger.

Triple Crown Publications presents

Chapter 3

After dropping Monica off at home, Anshon stopped by Constance's but she wouldn't let him in. "You not gonna let me in?" he asked, her in disbelief.

"No, I'm not. How long has it been since I've seen you? And what time is it? Eight o'clock in the morning," she said answering her own question, "Go back to that bitch you dropped off this morning and fuck her."

"How the fuck do you know who I dropped off?" Anshon reached his hand through the door and collared Constance. "Bitch are you trying to set me up? You know just a little too much for a bitch who don't never leave from around here."

"Get the fuck offa me!" she yelled pushing his hand down.

"Don't get killed fuckin' wit' the wrong nigga,"Anshon said, letting go of her. "Dumb bitch." She slammed the door in his face and he hopped back into his ride and took off.

Anshon was pissed. Who the hell did Constance think she was? He started to go back and kick in her door, but he changed his mind and instead made a few phone calls and put a hit on Tom-Tom's life.

Anshon called Tammy at least five or six times but she didn't answer. In his heart, he felt like something was wrong. He drove down Lizzie Street and pulled up in front of Teck and Wallo's house. He saw Fe-Fe leaving with Teck and a suitcase in her hand, "Where y'all goin'?" Anshon yelled out the window.

"This niggah done begged me to go to a program. I really ain't the one, but shit we'll see." Fe-Fe smiled at Anshon, "You know what I'm sayin'."

"It's all good Fe-Fe. " Anshon smiled, giving her a thumbs up. "Just see what happens."

"I'm taking care of that." Teck said, winking at Anshon. Anshon didn't know what to say. For a minute, he wondered if Teck was doing Fe-Fe. Anshon redialed Tammy on his cell phone and still there was no answer. He revved his engine to race over there and then he thought about the last time Tammy pulled a stunt and scared him half to death. He had to laugh. He picked up the phone and called Monica. "Wassup shawtie?"

"You," she yawned.

"Let me come scoop you."

"You just dropped me off," she laughed.

"I know, grab some gear you can shower at my spot. I wanna spend some time with you."

"Come on boy," she said in disbelief.

Anshon was there in less than five minutes. He beeped the horn and Monica came outside. She was already showered and changed. "Look at you cutie." Anshon kissed her on the cheek as she entered his car. Catching a quick peek of her ass, he shook his head. Just then, his phone rang. "Hello."

"Hey Anshon." It was Tammy. "I heard about what happened at the club last night, I can't believe that shit."

"Me either." Anshon shook his head thinking of Doughnut. "I feel sorry for Doughnut and Lexie's little girl."

"Yeah me too," Tammy said. "That's why I'ma drive

to Atlanta. I need to see my kids. Thank God for Aunt Rosa helping me out with them…Anshon."

"What's up Big Sis?"

"I'm moving." Tammy took a deep breath. "I need to be with my kids. These months without them have been hell. Aunt Rosa said I could stay with her. Plus, there's a hospital there with one of the best physical therapy clinics in the country. I could take physical therapy to get the strength back into my legs and be able to raise my kids again." Anshon felt like he wanted to cry, his sister was all he had. "I told you I was done with the game Anshon," Tammy continued, "Now it's time for me to get my life back."

"You couldn't tell me this in person?" he asked.

"No, because I didn't want to cry…like I am now," she whimpered.

"Big Sis, don't cry." Anshon couldn't look at Monica because he thought that he might break out in tears. Although Monica had only known Anshon for a night, she felt close to him. She took his free hand and placed it in her lap. He squeezed her thigh and smiled. The tears that he wasn't able to catch fell from his eyes.

"When are you leaving?" Anshon asked.

"Right now."

"What?!" Anshon screeched.

"I have to Anshon. Please I didn't wanna see you because I knew I would never be able to leave you."

Anshon's heart felt like it wanted to break, but he knew that as bad as he needed Tammy, he knew that her kids needed her more. And given the shit that went down with Tom-Tom at the pool hall, Anshon really didn't want Tammy anywhere around.

"I'ma miss you Tammy."

"I'ma miss you too, Anshon. I need you to send my things. All I can carry are a few pieces."

"You got that. I love you, Big Sis."

****

Constance paced back and forth in the living room of her apartment with her arms crossed and a mean look on her face. When she heard a motorcycle pull up she went to the door and unlocked it. Wallo came in and didn't pull off his helmet until he closed and locked the door behind him.

"What the fuck? Anshon came here a minute ago and grabbed me by the collar. I think he knows," Constance said in a panic.

"He don't know shit. Where's the cash and shit?"

"All over my damn living room, don't you see it?" He looked around and smiled. He moved toward Constance and began to rub her shoulders. She pushed him away. "Where have you been?"

"Somethin' came up." He gently grabbed her arm and turned her around.

"I'm so mad at you right now!" she snapped. "You be lettin' Teck talk to me any kinda way."

"Don't worry I've been getting on him about his mouth. I'm sorry baby." He unfolded her arms and placed them around his neck as he moved his arms around her waist. "I'ma make it up to you."

"I've heard that one before."

"You like your new car right?"

"Yeah and I'm worried about folks asking about my new car. I just made sergeant last week," she smiled.

"So?" He kissed her on the neck.

"So, people are wondering how I got a Benz so soon."

"Don't worry about that." He ran his hands through her auburn hair, "I love you girl."

She kissed him. "I'm ready to leave Selma."

"I know that baby." He continued to play in her hair. "Soon enough. Soon enough."

****

No sooner than Fe-Fe stepped foot in the drug rehab program did she turn around and come back out. "I'ma try to do this on my own," she said to Teck as she got back in the car. "Them niggas in there," she shook her head, "is some real goddamn crackheads. And if that's how I look I know I gotta kick this shit."

Teck bust out laughing. "Come on Fe-Fe, let's go home. I tell you what, if I catch you gettin' high, I'ma kick yo' ass."

"I can do it Teck," Fe-Fe assured him. "I just need somebody to believe in me."

"Well, I believe in you."

The first thing Teck made Fe-Fe do when they got back to her house was clean up. The house was just plain nasty and it didn't make any sense. Once she finished cleaning he sat her down and said, "I like you a lil' bit. You seem like you could be cool. But I ain't fuckin' you until you have an AIDS test. I don't give a damn, how good you look, AIDS don't have a face."

Fe-Fe sucked her teeth, but reluctantly agreed. "You gonna go on the block?" she asked not knowing, exactly what to say to him.

"Why?" He shrugged his shoulders.

"Because if you want to...you can sell from here. I can get the word out through the grapevine that you holding...and then you won't have to be all out in the open. It's just an idea, but I guess you gotta go see your girl or something."

"The first rule of the street," Teck said pulling Fe-Fe on the couch next to him, "is you can never get high off your own supply."

"What the hell is that suppose to mean?" she snapped.

"It means," he leaned over and kissed her on the forehead, "that if you fuck with my shit, we're done. And then I'ma kill you."

"Shut up, why you talking dumb?" Fe-Fe said. "I already told you that I ain't gonna get high no more."

"Ai'ight Lil' Bit, we'll see...and another thing I don't have a girl."

Fe-Fe's face lit up. She smiled and hugged him tight.

****

Two weeks passed and Tom-Tom was still nowhere to be found, Tammy was in Atlanta with her Aunt and her kids, Monica and Anshon were kickin' it hard, and Teck and Fe-Fe had locked down the block. Anshon was the connect, Teck cut up and distributed the weight, while Fe-Fe held the dough. Fe-Fe never asked Teck for anything extra. She took her AIDS test, as promised, and most of the money that she and Teck made, she took her cut and sent it to the cousin who took care of her twin boys.

Teck and Fe-Fe's sells were coming in like clock-work. Every fiend in Selma seemed to be knocking on Fe-Fe's door and nobody ever thought anything of it. At most, they thought that Teck was getting high with Fe-Fe, which is why he was there all the time. A few people noticed that Fe-Fe was starting to gain weight and was looking much cleaner, but her being sober was the last thing on anyone's mind.

That evening, around six o'clock, Teck told Fe-Fe he was down to his last and needed to re-up again.

"You need to chill for a minute," she said to him. "Jealous niggas might become suspicious."

Teck looked at Fe-Fe and thought about how good her advice had been up to now. "Ai'ight." He reached under her bed, pulled out his money box and started counting the dough they made today. He was sitting on a crate in her bedroom when he caught Fe-Fe staring at him.

"What you looking at girl?" he smiled.

"Nothing.," she said leaving out to go to the bathroom. As Fe-Fe walked out the room, Teck noticed a hole in the side of her jeans. Although he'd been enjoying her company, seeing her clothes with holes in them made him feel sorry for her.

She came back in the bedroom and sat on the mattress Indian style. Teck started staring at her. Her jet black wavy hair was wildly handing lose all over her shoulders. She shook it out and his dick instantly became hard. She smiled, knowing that he wanted to fuck her, but being a man of his word, he wouldn't dare touch her until her AIDS results came back. She smiled at him, the gleam from her front gold tooth, reflecting out of her mouth. "What?"

"I ain't say nothing," he said.

"Well, why you lookin' at me like that?"

"Cause I'm grown."

"Well, this my crib," she shot back.

"Oh," Teck laughed, "This here ain't our juke joint?"

"Nigga you crazy!" Fe-Fe fell out laughing.

Teck enjoyed her beauty even more, as she smiled. "Come on and take a ride with me," he said.

"Where we goin'?" she frowned.

"Damn, just come on, you'll see."

As they started driving, Fe-Fe asked him again, "Where we going?"

"Goldsboro," he said turning onto the highway.

"Who you know in Goldsboro? Going to re-up, huh? I see now that you don't know how to juice the game slow. To me it's like sex. Niggas wanna fuck fast and hustle fast and neither feels good. But if you hustle slow, you get a feel of it...just like pussy," Fe-Fe preached. *I betchu I'm waiting this long to fuck this hard headed nigga and his dick is fuckin' short and skinny*, she sighed to herself.

"Fe-Fe, I ain't goin' to re-up. We gonna get something to eat and get you some clothes."

"Say what!" Fe-Fe was stunned. She turned in the seat to face him. "Don't be playing no games with me

Teck. Why you trying to make me feel good, knowing damn well you gonna meet a square and ride pass me in the street this time next week. Just because I get high…well, use to get high…don't mean I don't have any feelings!" She felt like she wanted to cry. She folded her arms under her breasts, smacked her lips, and settled back in her seat. "I don't even know why I'm trippin' wit your young ass. You gonna be like the rest. Fuck you."

Teck glanced over at her as she looked out the tinted window. "If you would think sometimes before you run your mouth, you might make some sense."

She snapped her neck around. "Boy, please. I'm thirty-one years old. You only twenty-two. I know you don't like me, so you can kill this buying me clothes shit. All you want me to give you is some head anyway."

"Let me tell yo' ass one thing!" Teck said coming to a screeching halt in the middle of the highway, "I don't want you to suck my dick!"

Cars were passing by and blowing their horns. Fe-Fe was scared as hell. "Teck, please pull over to the shoulder, we're in the middle of the highway. Somebody could run into the back of us."

"Fuck all that!" he screamed. "You remind me so

much of my mother that every time I look at you I think of her. I want you to get clean. If I wanted you to suck my dick, then I would've stuck it down your throat the night Wallo and Doughnut were treating you like a hoe and running a train on you. I want you to get clean and do what my mother was never able to do!"

"What's that?" Fe-Fe said crying tears of joy and fright at the same time.

"Stay alive."

Fe-Fe was crying so bad that she couldn't talk. All she could do was hug him, nobody ever cared this much about her. Teck eased off the brake and slowly took off down the highway.

When they got to the mall, he handed her a thousand dollars. "Don't lose your damn mind," he warned. "The ten dollar spot got some cute shit. You ain't been shopping in Rich's and Belts, so don't start now." Before Fe-Fe could get a hold of herself, she'd planted a kiss on Teck's lips. He tapped her on the ass as she stepped out the car, "Buy some Tiger underwear."

Fe-Fe stayed in the mall for two hours. When she came back to the car, Teck was sleeping. "Wake up sleepyhead," she said. "Look at what I got."

"Show me when we get home. A nigga's hungry right now."

Fe-Fe grabbed Teck's arm and smiled as they started to pull off.

They stopped off at a local chicken and rib shack for some food.

"So, you gonna be my friend?" Fe-Fe asked as they ate.

"As long as you stay off that stuff." She held her head down. "Keep your head up Fe-Fe." Teck took his hand and lifted up her chin. "It's up to you to stay clean and let the past go. But I'ma do my part and you do yours…ok?"

"Yes." She nodded her head.

When they got back to Fe-Fe's house she couldn't wait to model the clothes for Teck. As she opened the front door, she saw that the mail had come. She took it out of the box and the first letter she saw was from the county health office. It had to be the results from her AIDS test. She grabbed it and ran into the bathroom, using the excuse of how bad she had to pee, so that Teck wouldn't suspect anything.

Carefully, she tore the test results open. She wondered if she would be punished for her fucked up life.

She took the letter out of the envelope and read it slowly:

Fendisha Lloyd the results of your HIV/AIDS test are negative.

Because of your high risk life style, please remember to be tested regularly.

"Thank you Jesus!" she shouted at the top of her lungs.

"Fe-Fe!" Teck banged on the bathroom door. "You okay?"

"I just got my AIDS test results." She snatched the door open. "Negative, Boo! Negative!"

She jumped in his arms, hugging him for dear life, while shoving the paper in his face. Glancing at the results, he said, "You making my dick hard, baby."

Massaging his hard on, she smiled. "Why don't we see what we can do about that."

Teck carried her into the bedroom. He laid her on the bed and then stood up. He cut the radio on and the D.J. was playing H-Town's classic, "Knockin' Da Boots."

"Damn...you look good, Fe-Fe." He got down on

the bed and climbed between her thighs, biting her nickel sized nipples through her shirt.

"Mmm, hum," she purred. "Teck, just be my friend, that's all I'll ask of you. Please, don't lie to me or try to play me."

"So, we a team?" he asked biting her nipples harder.

"Yes," she moaned, nodding her head.

He rolled to the side and unsnapped her bra. Her heavy double D's, practically smothered his face, but he was enjoying every minute of it. They fucked hard and long and called out each other's name as the sweet smell of sex filled the room. Each time he nutted, she would pull the rubber off and lick him like a kitten. And yes, he made sure she got her nut too. He fell asleep, as he laid behind her in the spoon position. Fe-Fe felt like a queen laying in Teck's arms, but deep in her heart, she felt it wouldn't last.

Chapter 4

The move to Atlanta was good for Tammy. Anshon missed her during the two months she'd been gone, but he and Monica were together everyday, so he didn't feel so bad. Tom-Tom was still missing but word on the street was that he was seen riding through Redwood Village apartments. Anshon knew it was only a matter of time before he would catch up to him.

"Hey baby," Anshon greeted Monica, who laid across the floor studying for her college finals.

"Hey sugar sweets," Monica said rolling on her back. "You just gettin' here?"

"Yeah, I missed you." He pushed her schoolbooks to the side and laid on top of her.

"Mmm...I know your girl gets the best," Monica hissed.

79

"Don't play me mami," Anshon said in his best Latin accent. "You know what I give you is better than what my girl gets."

Monica mushed Anshon on the side of his head. "Don't play with me!"

Anshon laughed as he started feeling between her legs.

Over at Fe-Fe's, Teck was sweeping the kitchen floor as Fe-Fe stood at the stove frying some chicken. "What time tomorrow will the new furniture be here?" she said over her shoulder. Not only was she excited about the new digs for her crib but she was even more excited about her new life. It wasn't everyday that a crackhead was given a second chance. As far as Fe-Fe was concerned, Teck was *that* nigga.

"The furtniture'll be here in the morning, baby," Teck said, dumping the dust pan into the garbage. "At least by ten."

The sound of Teck calling Fe-Fe "baby" was the sweetest sound Fe-Fe had heard in a long time. Leaning up against the counter, Teck pulled out a wad of cash he made that day and started counting it. Afterwards, he handed it to her and said, "Put that away. Send half of it to your cousin for your sons and the other half, I want you to open up a bank account."

Fe-Fe couldn't believe her ears. She finished cooking the chicken and fixed Teck a plate of food. After they had dinner, she led him by the hand into her candle-lit bedroom.

"Teck," she said kissing his pecks, slowly laying with him on the bed, and sucking on his nipples, "I swear you the best man I've ever had. I never had nobody to care about me."

He rolled on top of her. "Don't worry about that no more. Just know that I care about you. Now enough of the sentimental shit. I wanna hear this headboard bang against the wall!"

Fe-Fe fell out laughing and before Teck knew it she'd rolled him over and slid between his legs, took his dick into her mouth, and was slowly gettin' her eagle on. He let his head roll back and in between seeing stars, he could swear that her tongue felt better than a hot and wet prison wash rag coated with melted Vaseline.

****

"Yo, Shon, whut up?" Teck called Anshon on his cell phone, trying to set up a time to re-up. "You got a lil' freak in the secret Bat Cave or what?"

"Naw, I don't fuck with freaks. But since you tryin'

to find out what my dick's been up to, I been chillin' with that lil' shawtie, Monica, from the club. Wassup wit you?" Anshon asked.

"Doin' my ting ting. Dawg, tryin' to re-up, na'mean?"

"I feel you, but yo' Teck..." Anshon hesitated, "I ain't tryin' to be in your business, but you know you can't get high off your own supply."

"What the hell you talkin' about?"

"This shit you got goin' on with Fe-Fe. Yo, you ain't on that shit is you?"

"Maaaaannn, hell naw. Fe-Fe is clean Dawg. Have you seen her lately? She lookin' good as hell, her gold tooth shinnin'; don't sleep on Fe. Fuck what dem niggas in the street sayin'."

"Ai'ight, I'll call you later. We can meet up about five or six this evening."

****

Tom-Tom sat in his beat up and rusted trailer in Buck Adams trailer park, laid out on his couch smoking a Newport, playing with his dick, and watching TV. Nothing was going right. He had no money, his food was getting low, and Anshon had a price on his head.

He put his dick back in his pants, sat up, and started snorting a line of coke. Slowly but surely, Tom-Tom was falling off. He either had to come out of hiding or die. He couldn't believe what was happening to him. How did the little boy that he helped raise become the one to have a price on his head. After all, Tom-Tom was the one who taught Tammy the game and she passed it on to Anshon. "I made you ma'fucker!" Tom-Tom yelled out as his high started to take affect.

"I'm the fuckin' star!" Tom started thinking about Tammy. "Cripple bitch!" He took his index finger, held his right nostril closed, and snorted a line of coke with the open one. Thoughts of Tammy raced through his mind.

After Tom-Tom left Tammy she called him and cried for a month, begging him to come back. But he couldn't. How could he when she had risen to the top of the game and refused to move over?

"Together?" he said to her, the day he got out of prison, "Bitch is you crazy?"

"But how can I give all this up?" she cried, "I've worked too hard. Look baby, I got two female drivers to run the D.C. line and all you basically have to do is chill and watch the dough roll in."

"Naw, you think I'ma let a bitch led me around in

the game. You done lost your mind? I'm the one that put you on. Know what, fuck it and fuck you!" It's not that he didn't love Tammy but his heart couldn't take the way she ran the game without him. A quiet, red-head, freckle-faced, two dollar waitress was slangin' dem thangs better then he could've ever imagined and to make matters worst everybody that she was sellin' to wanted to keep it that way.

That's when Tom-Tom hooked up with Teck and Wallo. He'd heard through the streets that they were stick up kids, the Dirty-Dirty's version of the old DMX, robbin' niggas, and bragging about it. He hooked up with them and came up with a plan: snatch Tammy's cash and force her to start over. Then he would regain the hustle and the bitch, Tammy, would fall back into her place.

But he never imagined that the robbery would go bust and Tammy would be shot in Redwood Village parking lot. So, the combination of Tom-Tom, Teck, and Wallo stayed on the low, until the night in the pool hall. That was supposed to be their coming out party. They just never expected that Doughnut was such a crazy motherfucker.

"I swear to God I'ma kill that bitch!" Tom-Tom said, laying his head back and watching the ceiling. "I'ma kill her!"

Chapter 5

An hour later Tom-Tom was coming down from his high. He looked out the window and then it clicked. He knew just what to do to teach Tammy a lesson.

He walked outside to the shed in his backyard and took out three bottles of lighter fluid along with a box of matches. "I'ma teach this bitch not to ever fuck with me!" He jumped in his car and drove over to Tammy's house. Once he got there, he remembered that the gate was controlled by a numeric code, but Tom-Tom was sure that Tammy hadn't changed so he punched in their daughter's birth date. The gate popped open. He drove up close to the house and pulled his car around back. He took the lighter fluid and started to splash it around the foundation of the house. "This bitch thinks that she runnin' shit! I'll fix her. Sleep well, ya mute legged bitch!" Tom-Tom sneered, convinced that

Tammy was in the house. "Sleep all night and burn in hell." By the time Tom-Tom was done, he'd emptied three bottles of lighter fluid. Then he stood back, pulled a Newport from behind his ear, and lit it. He took a drag and flicked it onto the grass. The fire blazed instantly, giving Tom-Tom little time to take off.

Anshon and Monica laid across the floor after two hours of hard fuckin' when his cell phone rang. "I hope your bitch ass sister's dope dealin' house burns to the ground and I hope she sleeps well in it!" a sinister voice said.

Anshon repeated those threatening words in his head. The number appeared on his Caller ID as unknown and he kept trying to put it all together. "Oh shit, Monica!" Anshon said, "My sister's house! I gotta go check on her house."

Monica was in a panic watching Anshon throw his clothes on. "What's wrong Baby?"

"Nothing," he said, zipping his jeans. "I gotta go check on my sister's house."

Anshon jumped in his car and called Teck. He didn't get an answer, then he called Wallo. "Whut up, Anshon," Wallo yawned. He'd been out runnin' trains all night.

"Nigga get dressed and meet me outside. I think that fuckin' Tom-Tom has done something to my sister's house."

Wallo rolled his eyes in his head. He prayed that Tom-Tom wasn't turning out to be like Doughnut's crazy ass. "Ai'ight." Wallo took a deep breath, "Come through."

Anshon picked up Wallo and headed up to Tammy's. When he got there all he could see were blazes of fire and smoke. The firemen wouldn't let anyone get close. "Goddamn!" Anshon threw a punch in the air, "My sister could've been in that bitch!" He turned to Wallo, "I know it was that bitch ass faggot, Tom-Tom!"

"Let's go kick his ass!" Wallo said, pissed off that Tom-Tom would do some dumb shit like this. "Let's go get Teck first."

"Where he at?" Anshon asked, jumping back in his car.

"Where else? Fe-Fe's."

Anshon and Wallo practically flew to Fe-Fe's. They told Teck the story and he rolled out with them. As the screen door was still swinging against the frame from Teck leaving, Fe-Fe's heart started to race as she thought about what they might do to Tom-Tom. She prayed that they all came back home alive.

Tom-Tom was in his kitchen paranoid, from the coke he snorted. He kept looking out the window and thinking that the police were coming to arrest him. "This is some fuckin' bullshit!" he muttered to himself heading back into the living room. He stopped in his tracks heading back to peek out the kitchen window and hoped that Tammy's death would make the news. "See you in hell, bitch!" he laughed walking back into the living room. He flopped down on his sofa and kicked his feet up on the armrest and closed his eyes. He was dozing off when he heard a car pull up outside. His heart skipped a beat as Anshon, Teck, and Wallo shot up his door. He jumped from the couch and took cover, "What the fuck!"

Wallo walked over to Tom-Tom and threw him on the sofa. "Stupid ass!" Tom-Tom tussled with Wallo.

"Yo," Tom-Tom stuttered, "I-I-I didn't do nu-nu-nuthin'." Anshon and Teck broke them apart. Tom-Tom wasn't a small dude and one on one he would have fucked Wallo up. But Tom-Tom knew he was 'bout to get jumped if he overtook Wallo so instead Tom-Tom tried to make a break for his .38. Teck punched him in the jaw as Anshon came from behind and put a choke-hold on him.

"Calm down nigga!" Anshon hissed in his ear. Tom-Tom continued to struggle with Anshon as Teck and Wallo started raining blows to his face. Anshon wrapped his leg around one of Tom-Tom's and tripped him up. When he was on the floor gasping for air, Anshon pointed the .9mm to his head. Tom-Tom rolled to his back as Wallo kicked him in the ribs. Blood ran freely from Tom-Tom's busted lip. As Teck went to pick up Tom-Tom and throw him across the room, he peeked four bottles of lighter fluid and matches. "Bingo!" Teck said pointing to the evidence.

"Man I ain't-" Tom-Tom tried to speak, but was cut off by Wallo's left foot to the side of his head.

"Shut up, fuckin' snitch ass lame!" Wallo yelled.

"Strip!" Anshon said kicking Tom-Tom in the leg. "Get naked punk!"

"Fuck you!" Tom-Tom shot back. "You ain't no killer!"

Anshon smiled then nodded at Teck who started to put some duct tape around Tom-Tom's wrist and ankles. Tom-Tom started to struggle, but ceased when Wallo pulled out a box cutter and put the blade to his throat. Once his ankles were tightly taped and the same for his hands behind his back, Wallo then used the box cutter to cut his clothes off.

"Don't cut the lame!" Teck said as Wallo nicked Tom-Tom for the third time. Tom-Tom was scared now. He was butt ass naked and couldn't do shit.

"Hold the fuck still!" Anshon said to Tom-Tom as Teck pulled out a Magic Marker and wrote DEAD NIGGA on Tom-Tom's forehead. He started to cry and mumble. Wallo planted a boot in his stomach then kicked him in the head.

"Now you gonna know what Cain felt like. Pick his bitch ass up!"

Tom-Tom pleaded with Anshon. "Yo man, chill. I'll leave town...I'll do whatever man...yo Anshon!" he shouted. Anshon ignored him. "Man, Please!" Tom-Tom shouted falling to his knees. Snot ran from his nose as he started to crumble. "Please man...I didn't mean to do it," he sobbed. "Look, I raised you Anshon. I taught Tammy the game, she stole my shit. Teck, Wallo,   tell'em.
Tell 'em."

"Shut the fuck up!" Wallo shouted.

Teck answered by kicking him in the mouth.

"I got something for your ass!" Anshon said, running back to his car. He remembered that Monica left her overnight bag in his car. He went in the bag and pulled out a big electric curling iron. When Anshon returned back to the house Tom-Tom snickered. He thought Anshon was going to come back with a gun and kill him. But he never expected a curling iron. Anshon walked in and picked up the lighter fluid, then he walked over to Tom-Tom, who Wallo now had in a choke hold. He took the lighter fluid, poured the whole bottle on top of the curler and shoved it up Tom-Tom's ass. Tom-Tom started to scream, as Anshon started pushing the curler further into his asshole. Teck grabbed an extension cord from the floor, swung it in front of Tom-Tom's face, like a pocket watch and threw it to Wallo, who plugged the iron into the socket. Tom-Tom shitted on himself. The curling iron was making snap, crackle, and pop noises up Tom-Tom's ass. He dropped his head, slob sliding out the side of his mouth, and fainted—never to wake up again.

"Die slow ma'fucker!" Anshon said as he, Teck, and Wallo, headed out the door, "And that's on the strength of my sister!"

"Boy, what happened to you?" Fe-Fe said looking at Teck's ripped and blood splattered jacket. To afraid to know what really happened she retracted her question. "Ain't no need in tellin' me."

"No matter what happens," Teck said to Fe-Fe, flopping down on the bed next to her, "always know that I really care for you."

"Boy," Fe-Fe said, feeling the lump rising in her throat, "be quiet."

"Hey Fe," Teck said, after a few minutes of silence. "I got something for you." He went in the bedroom and came back out. "Here." He handed her a diamond bracelet.

"Oh my Lord! Teck," Fe-Fe squealed. "Jesus!" She started hugging him tight. "What happened to the box baby?"

"I...I...I don't know," Teck stuttered "Just accept the gift Fe, damn."

"I'll take this gift, if you can take mine."

"What?" Teck smiled, watching Fe-Fe unbuckle his pants.

"This," she said as she started giving him head.

"Damn," Teck mumbled, "I should've given you this bracelet a long time ago..."

Chapter 6

Anshon was glad the sun was out today. He was at a stoplight on New Bern Avenue when he dropped the top with Slick Rick's "Hey Young World" massaging the four 12s in the trunk. He called Monica, hoping that she was up. She picked up on the second ring.

"What up shawtie, let me come scoop you."

"Anshon, you heard what happened to Tom-Tom?" she asked.

From Monica's tone, he didn't know if she were asking him or telling him. "Is that a question?" he asked.

"Yeah."

"Oh. Naw," he said. "I ain't heard nothin'."

"He was electrocuted. His insides were outside of his body by the time the police found him. You know anything about that?"

"Come on now shawtie. What I look like? I can't say that I feel bad, about the nigga being dead...I mean my sister may feel some kinda way...but hell we all gotta die sometime."

"Whatever Anshon."

"Yo', I'm tryin' to see you. Wassup?"

She sucked her teeth and blushed at the same time. "Come on boy."

Anshon smiled. "Fe-Fe and Teck are having a small card party later on. So I hope you know how to put your Spade game down."

****

"My book!" Fe-Fe yelled at Teck, grinning.

Teck did a double take. "Baby," he said, not wanting to embarrass her in front of Monica and Anshon. "Where's your other cap at?" He pointed to her mouth.

"I wanted to surprise you. I got implants, one porcelain and one gold."

"Let me see," Monica said to Fe-Fe. "You look good girl!"

"Thank you," Fe-Fe said, covering her mouth. As she did that her present from Teck slid down her arm.

"Wow Fe-Fe!" Monica screamed. Anshon and Teck looked at her like she was crazy. "That bracelet is beautiful! Let me see."

"Teck gave it to me." Fe-Fe held her arm out.

Monica looked at the bracelet and her eyes lit up, "This is mine! Where did you get this from Teck?"

"This ain't yours," Fe-Fe said snatching her arm back. "My man gave me this."

"That is mine!" Monica said, "My name is engraved on the lock. Look at it closely. That's my bracelet that I was jacked for that night in the club."

Fe-Fe took off the bracelet and looked at the lobster claw lock and it read Monica. Fe-Fe felt like a fool, she looked at Teck. "I thought this was the jewelers inscription. I'm sorry Monica...I though maybe I had a name brand piece."

"I can't believe this shit," Teck said, looking at Anshon, who had his face twisted.

"I brought that shit from the pawn shop. I would've never known that it was stolen." He took the bracelet out of Fe-Fe's hands and gave it to Monica. "Here you go baby girl. My fault." He turned to Fe, "I'll get you another one."

Fe-Fe sat back down in her chair embarrassed. This was one time that she wished she was still getting high.

"Girl, you hear what happened to Tom-Tom?" Monica said, trying to break the uncomfortable silence.

"Naw, what?" Fe-Fe mumbled, peeking at the bracelet that was now on Monica's wrist.

"My home girl, Gina," Monica said, "called me this morning and told me that Tom-Tom's next door neighbor, found him electrocuted. The insides of his ass were on his living room floor."

"What!!!" Fe-Fe screeched, looking at Teck. "Who done it?"

"I don't know," Teck frowned, "what the fuck is you, the law? Don't be looking at me."

Fe-Fe looked at Anshon. He simply turned his head. Fe-Fe sucked her teeth, grabbed the deck of cards and reshuffled them.

"Anshon?" Monica said, "You seen my electric curling iron? I left it in your car."

Anshon spit his beer out. Teck looked at him and handed him a napkin. "What the hell kinda question is that?" he asked, "I don't keep up with no damn curlers."

"It ain't that deep, Anshon. I just asked."

"Well naw," he snapped, "I ain't seen 'em."

The card game was down hill from there. They finished the hand they were playing and then Anshon started yawning. "I'm getting a little tired. We'll get up with y'all tomorrow," he said looking at Monica.

Monica lifted her arms in the air and stretched. "Okay baby."

"Well, I'm glad y'all came by," Fe-Fe said. They all stood up from the table and walked toward the front door. Anshon and Teck walked outside to Anshon's car, while the girls lagged behind.

"Fe-Fe," Monica said, grabbing her hand. "I got something for you." She handed her the bracelet.

"What you doing Monica?" Fe-Fe was surprised and tried pushing the bracelet back into Monica's hands. "This yours."

"You can have it," Monica smiled. "The diamonds ain't real and the gold is just ten carat. I don't need it. You take it."

Fe-Fe didn't know what to say. She kissed Monica on the cheek. "Nobody never gave me nothing. Anything I ever had came cause I sucked dick real good or I stole it. So thank you, I really appreciate it, but it's yours and I don't want it. Please take it back."

Monica could tell that she was making Fe-Fe feel uncomfortable. "Okay Fe-Fe, but the next time, I want you to take what I give you."

"I will…"Monica kissed Fe-Fe on the cheek and she and Anshon left.

****

The next morning Teck and Fe-Fe were bagging up coke when Fe-Fe asked, "You think Anshon killed Tom-Tom?"

Teck picked up two grams off the table and rolled them in the palm of his hand, making sure they were the same size. He placed them back on the table then carefully picked up a razor. Fe-Fe repeated her question.

"Yo, check this," Teck snapped, "you see I'm tryin'

to handle this." He pointed to the coke. "Just mind your business and handle this trap right here. This lil' spot is all we got to worry 'bout. I gotta wrist fulla rubber bands, which equals mo' money and mo' problems, and that's more than enough to have on your mind. Don't worry about what happened to Tom-Tom."

"I understand." Fe-Fe smirked, "I understand quiet well. Anshon ain't kill him. Both y'all did!"

Teck ignored her and continued bagging up his work.

An hour later, Teck finished and said to Fe-Fe, who was serving a fiend and listening to All My Children, "I gotta roll real quick. I need to go and check my brother."

Fe-Fe nodded her head as Teck left out the back door.

****

It was ten o'clock in the morning; Anshon had just dropped Monica off for her morning classes at the community college. He started to run home but then he decided to go by Fe-Fe's and check Teck.

"Yo Fe," Anshon called, rattling the screen on the front door.

Fe-Fe didn't hear Anshon announce himself, but she heard the door rattle. She ran to the front door hoping it was Teck. She'd been unable to sleep every since she found a bloody ski mask tucked under her bed, along with five different IDs, from people that she knew lived on the other side of Selma. *"I hope this nigga ain't runnin' no credit card scheme,"* she thought on her way to the door. *"Shit, if white folks locked Martha Stewart up, niggas can forget about it. It's pretty much a wrap, cause in a moment lynching gon' be legal, so I know Teck got better sense then to be messing with white collar crime shit. He better stick to the nickel and dime, state charges.* "Teck," she yelled snatching the front door open, "What is this shit I found?" She held the ski mask out. When she saw Anshon was at the door, she quickly snatched it back. "Anshon," she said breathing heavy, "I thought you were Teck."

Anshon was so taken aback by Fe-Fe, that he never noticed the mask. She was dressed in a tight white turtleneck that hugged her heavy breasts. Her nipples were hard, slightly poked out through her bra, causing the imprint to come through her shirt. She also had on a tight pair of Never Broke jeans that Teck brought her.

Anshon wanted to grab his dick. It was so hard that it was starting to ache. For the first time, Anshon knew that as long as she was sober, he could imagine fuck-ing her.

Fe-Fe turned her back to him, "Close the door behind you."

Immediately, his eyes went to her ass. He had no choice but to grab his dick. Her ass resembled a brand new pumped up basketball.

Fe-Fe sat down on the couch and Anshon went to sit next to her.

"Where's Teck?" Anshon asked, trying to cover up his hard-on as he sat.

"Good question." Fe-Fe reached over Anshon and grabbed the cordless phone, her 36-D's brushing back and forth across his dick. She dialed Teck's number...no answer. "Fuck this. I was gonna cook, but ain't no tellin' when his ass gonna get here. Can you take me to McDonald's right quick?"

"Yeah," Anshon said standing up, he placed his hands in his jeans pocket, hoping to somehow hide his hard-on again. "I can go for a few bacon, egg and cheese sausage biscuits...and some fries."

Fe-Fe went upstairs to get her purse and left a note for Teck that she went to McDonald's with Anshon.

"It's cold as hell out here," Fe-Fe said as she got into the Chevy. "I'll be glad when it's summertime."

"Me too," Anshon replied. "I wonder if Teck and Wallo gon' be selling them dinners again?"

"Your guess is as good as mine," Fe-Fe said, looking out the window.

Anshon took I-95 then rode it until he reached the rest stop. This McDonald's was closer that than the one in the center of town. They went through the McDonald's driveway and twenty minutes later, they had the food and were back at Fe-Fe's house. Teck still hadn't returned.

"How old are you?" Fe-Fe asked Anshon as they sat in the living room eating their food.

"Twenty-two, why?"

"Just askin'," she said balling up the wrapper from her sausage biscuit. "Hey, I got another question to ask." She took a sip of her diet coke.

"Yeah?"

"Let's say...if you was to like...um...to meet me out of town and didn't know me, would you step to me?"

Anshon had a mouth full of food and quickly

picked up his cup of Sprite to wash it down. "I'ma act like I didn't hear that Fe-Fe."

She rolled her eyes. "Fool, I ain't tryin' to do nothin' wit you. I just wanna know if you would find me good to look at...that's all."

"Oh...well...if I had never met you and didn't knew your past...then hell yeah I'd step to you with the quickness. Why you ask?"

"Cause your dick was hard, when I reached over you for the phone earlier," Fe-Fe smiled, pushing her wavy hair behind her ears.

"You trippin' Fe-Fe," he said removing the wrapper from his third biscuit. He peeked at her from outta the corner of his eye, he hated that she knew his dick was hard. But hell, ever since she's been clean, she was something to look at, 5'3", 36-D, 26-38, 140 lbs. She was turning a lot of heads and most like, Anshon were ashamed to admit it. Fe-Fe was just a coal covered diamond that needed to be polished and Teck happened to be the only one to see that she was a rare jewel. Niggas that had tricked Fe-Fe knew how good the pussy was and a few were now hating Teck because he had Fe-Fe on lock. He glanced over at Fe-Fe to see if she were still looking at him.

"Let me stop," she laughed.

"Ai'ight." Anshon stood to leave. "Tell Teck to call me."

As he went to step out the door, Fe-Fe called out his name. "Anshon, thanks for not puttin' dirt on my name. I know you could of told Teck about me tryin' to give you some ass that night when I was trickin' with Bobby at Masters Inn. I know it was before me and him hooked up...but you know how it would look." She hunched her shoulders. "Teck would start thinkin' we up to somethin'."

"That's the past, Fe-Fe and you still cool wit me. Just have Teck call me when he get in."

"O.K." Fe-Fe blushed, closing the door behind him.

****

A week had passed and still no Teck. Fe-Fe was starting to give up on their relationship.

She was cleaning her living room when she found a shit load of jewelry underneath her couch and more stolen ID's. *What the fuck is going on here?* she thought to herself. She was holding the jewelry in her hand when Teck walked in. She quickly threw it back under the couch. When she looked up Teck was standing over her.

"What you lookin' for?" he asked.

"Nuthin'," she snapped. "Where the fuck you been?"

"Out!"

"Well since you been out, you can stay the fuck out! Nigga, I'm sick of y'all big dick ma'fuckahs that think you runnin' shit. You ain't runnin' shit for me! Fuck you!"

Fe-Fe was going off so bad that Teck couldn't get a word in. "Wait a minute, Fe-."

"No, you wait a minute nigga. Punk-bitch-ass-cripple-eyed-ma'fucker!"

"Look, I'm sorry ai'ight? Come on, I was buggin'. I should've called, but I didn't."

"Nope." She twisted her lips. "Not workin'! Plus niggah she said, reaching under the couch and throwing the jewelry at him. I'm finding more goddamn goods than drugs. What the fuck is really going on? You robbin' niggas? You a stick up kid?"

"Hell no!" Teck snapped. "How the hell you just gon' say some shit like that to me? Fuck it, Fe, if it's that deep fuck it. That's my grandmother's shit. I was hiding it under the couch because I was gon' give it to you."

"Yeah, just like that fuckin' bracelet you embarrassed the shit outta me with! Whatever nigga. Whatever!"

"Ai'ight I see you done got clean and lost your fuckin' mind. Remember I got you out the gutter. You ain't shit but a tramp ass trash! I made you, you just a squirrel tryna get a nut."

"Look at you, you Orange Juice Jones wanna be ma'fucker! You ain't made me. If anything I made your no gamin' ass. If the hustle was left up to you, you'd be in jail for a fuckin' dime piece. You ain't Federal weight yet niggah. Ya better slow the fuck down, fo' you get sprayed the fuck down!"

"Sprayed? Oh now you gon' shoot me?" Teck couldn't help but laugh. He was laughing so hard that before he knew anything Fe-Fe was laughing.

"Ain't shit funny," she pouted, folding her arms across her breast. Teck walked over and hugged her.

"I'm sorry Fe, for real. You gotta forgive ya man."

Fe-Fe looked at Teck and couldn't help but to forgive him. She turned around and hugged him. He kissed her and she melted in his arms.

Chapter 7

Constance was in the back seat of her Mercedes pulling up her satin panties after giving it up to her baby's father, Wallo. They were parked in the bus parking lot behind a few school buses at Selma Middle School. When she was fully dressed, she slid over to him and kissed him deeply for close to five minutes.

"A few more months and we can blow this place," he said zipping up his jeans.

"I hope so. I'm sick of working at that prison," she said climbing up to the front seat. "Hey!" she giggled when he squeezed her butt. He got out and stretched his body then opened her front door to get his helmet. Again, she leaned over to kiss him before he left. She sat and waited until he got on his Ninja ZX-10R. "I love you." She shouted over the roar of the motorcycle as he revved up the engine before doing a short burnout.

Teck came home at 10:38 p.m. to find Fe-Fe wide-awake on the couch looking at TV. Before she could flip on him, he pulled out a hand full of crumpled bills, "I been hustling all day."

"Yeah right," Fe-Fe sucked her teeth, "where?"

"In Durham. There's this van that one of my home-boys told me about. And that's where I was. Me and Wallo hopped this van and they took us to a spot to slang."

"Niggah who is you talkin' to?" Fe-Fe started laughing, "That shit you just said is crazier than a mother-fuckah. Ain't nobody but 5-0 promisin' niggas pipe dreams; like I should believe that a goddamn van gon' take you to slang."

"Ai'ight, Fe," Teck said, realizing how ridiculous he was sounding. "You got that. I was just doing some things that I don't wanna involve you in...but come on Boo," he said holding her close and kissing her neck, "Anything I do is for me and you."

"I'm pissed at you boy!"

"Why?" he twisted his face." 'Cause I been out draggin' my ass for you? Other niggas stay out to two or three in the mornin' and some don't even come in at all. And it's what," he glanced at his watch, "10:45 and you trippin'. I could'a reed up and stayed wit some project chic in Durham, but I cut it short and brought my ass home to you!"

****

Anshon was on his knees leaning forward braced up on one arm as he used his other arm to hold Monica's legs, both legs, on the right side of his shoulder as he fucked her on her living room floor in front of the TV. Each time he drove into her, it sent her hands to a different part of his body. His neck, shoulders, chest, waist, wrist, ass; over and over he sought to immerse his entire body inside her. She had already chanted out his name over a hundred times. It went both ways. He couldn't get enough of her as he switched positions for the fifth time. Her nipples were already sore from his mouth.

"ANSHON!"

"MONICA!"

They said each other's name as she reached back to spread her ass open for him. The sight of her ass spread with her cheeks apart for him nearly caused him to explode in the condom. He held back and slowly slid back into her pussy.

"Pussy...so...fuckin'...good!" he said through clenched teeth as he watched her butt quiver like jello. The rhythm had her pussy talking as she cried out his name in a feverish lust. Suddenly, they both felt the condom pop. "Ohhh baby," he moaned at the sweet feeling of being inside of her raw. She slowly slid off his dick then pulled the busted condom off. Her lips quivered as he rubbed his throbbing dick against her swollen labia. She fell to her elbows arching her pussy higher in the air. Anshon flipped her over and placed his mouth back on her breasts as she reached down to massage his dick. She could feel the blood throbbing through his veins.

"Mmmmm baby," she cried as she crossed her legs over his back and pulled him inside her. Anshon lost all control as he started pumping her. Monica was talking and mumbling incoherently as Anshon drove deeper into her causing their sweaty naked bodies to smack together. She moved his face towards hers for a passionate kiss. Each thrust made him pick up his speed. He came up on his arms, driving deeper, stronger, and harder into her sweet pussy until he exploded deep inside her.

Anshon lost count of the number of times he nutted inside her, once the condom broke. He couldn't believe that he had slipped up and ate pussy till she glazed his face...not once, but twice. The only problem was when he was eating her pussy, he kept imaging that it was Fe-Fe's clit he was sucking on. That made him grind his tongue faster and not until he brought Monica to a triple orgasm did he realize that he'd been totally out of his mind.

After sex, Monica and Anshon rolled over and went to sleep. They didn't wake up until midnight when Anshon's phone started ringing. He reached over from the bed hitting the button for the speaker phone.

"Dawg, you up?" It was Teck.

"Um..Wassup?" Anshon said with his eyes closed.

"You high or something?"

"Pimp please, full night," Anshon muttered rubbing his neck.

"Yo, I'ma 'bout to dip to Goldsboro with Fe-Fe, I'ma take'er to the movies. She told me you wanted me to call."

"I was tryin' to see what was up with you. Where you bounce to?"

"I was just chillin'. Well dawg, I'm out. Sound like you in the bed, I'll holla."

As Anshon laid back down the phone rang again. This time he snatched it off the receiver. "Speak to a pimp-nigga," Anshon said, flipping his phone open.

"Pimp nigga?" Tammy frowned. "Oh hell no!"

"Big Sis!" Anshon sat up in the bed, "Wassup?"

"I met a man, boy?"

"For real?" Anshon smiled. "What's his name and address in case I have to bust his ass."

"Be quiet she giggled. His name is Victor, he's a good guy. But look," Tammy's tone changed from silly to serious, "I hear it's a lotta niggas getting robbed and shit in Selma, Raleigh, and Durham. Even Goldsboro. It's time to give it a rest Anshon. The South ain't safe no more."

"What is you?" Anshon smirked, "Young Buck? The south ain't safe no more, so what? Get a gun? Well I got three or four!"

If Tammy could come through the phone and kick Anshon's ass she would've. "When are you going to learn that this hustlin' shit is a dead end, huh? You save any money, Anshon? You have any cash in the bank? Or is Monica sportin' every fuckin' name brand in the world. Is the double wide that goddamn laid. Get out the game. Please, it ain't worth it. Look at me, I'm still fighting. I can't even take care of my kids without help."

"Oh here you go with that bullshit. Tammy ain't nothin' wrong with you, you met a man didn't you?"

"Nigga, I met some dick."

"Tammy-"

"No, be quiet Anshon and listen. I met a man, but what does that have to do with you being safe. Roll out Anshon. Ma'fuckers is showin' up dead all over the place. Niggas is gettin' robbed."

"Being robbed don't equal being dead," Anshon snapped.

"Anshon, don't be stupid. All you gotta do is buck and you done."

"Anyway," Anshon said, changing the subject, "how's my niece and nephew?"

Tammy wanted to come through the phone and strangle Anshon. She took a deep breath. "They're fine. Starting to ask questions about their sorry ass daddy. When I come back to Selma I may just have to talk to him about seeing his kids."

"Tammy…" Anshon swallowed hard.

"What?"

"Tom-Tom…is dead."

She dropped the phone and Anshon could hear her screaming in the background. "This is what I'm talking about! This is it! What! What! How?" she said picking the phone back up. "Please don't tell me that you, you…did it!"

"What the hell? Please, Tammy. I'm not answering that."

"I gotta come home." Tammy cried. "I need to see what I can find in my house; maybe some pictures or something for my kids. Maybe I can get by to see his mother. I know she's torn up."

"Tammy," Anshon signed, "there was a fire."

"What? What does that mean?"

"Your house was burned down. Everybody thinks that Tom-Tom did it."

"I'm on my way," Tammy cried, hanging up the phone, "I'm on my way."

Anshon hung up with Tammy, took a quick shower, slipped on his jeans, hoddy, and skull cap. He grabbed his heat and car keys. "Monica," he nudged her a little.

She cracked her eyes open. "Hmm."

"I'll be back later. It's some money on the dresser if you wanna go out. Otherwise, chill here until I come back. Ai'ight?"

"Ai'ight Anshon."

For some reason Anshon's heart was beating fast as he drove over to Teck and Fe-Fe's. He wondered why Wallo was always missing in action whenever some shit went down and his mind started to wonder if Wallo was throwing some salt in the game. *And what about Tom-Tom,* Anshon thought, *what was that nigga talking about?*

Instead of heading down Lizzie Street, Anshon made a right into Redwood Village apartments, to pay Constance a visit. When he pulled up, he saw Wallo's motorcycle parked in her parking spot. "Ai'ight," Anshon swallowed hard, "It's all good, cuz when ya get down to it, pussy is all the same."

He knocked on Constance's door, light at first, until he thought he heard what sounded like fucking sounds come through the crack of the door. After that, Anshon started kicking the door.

Wallo jumped, he was getting his dick sucked and whoever the visitor was they'd picked a fucked up time to come. "What the fuck?" Wallo said, looking towards the door. Anshon kicked it again.

Constance unwrapped her lips and wiped her mouth with the back of her hand. Wallo zipped his pants up, but he couldn't erase the attitude off his face.

"What?" Constance snapped at Anshon, when she opened the door. "Where's your little seventeen-year-old college groupie?"

"Why you all in my business? What, you wanna suck two dicks? Go find ya kid's father and bust a nut in that niggas mouth, since you dying to be a hoe."

Wallo snatched the door completely open and looked at Anshon, "Yo' Shon," he looked serious, "Don't try and play me crazy. Don't be disrespecting her."

"Oh my fault," Anshon said, seething, "I ain't know this was your hoe now. I thought we was better than that."

"Better than what?" Wallo snapped.

"Than you fuckin' my ex-chicks."

"Yo," Wallo laughed, "this my daughter's moms. You the one stepped outta line son. I ain't call you on it, cause we weren't together. Just like, I use to bang

Monica, but you ain't need to know that. Not every nigga waking around should be showing his hand. Na'mean?"

"Monica?" Anshon placed his hand on the butt of his gun.

"Chill," Constance pleaded. She knew better than Anshon how much Wallo really hated him. "Just go Anshon."

"Fuck leavin'." Wallo stepped closer to Anshon. "What you come over here for?"

"Oh nigga you really don't want it with me, so you better back the fuck up."

"Whatever," Wallo said, blowing out air.

"Fuck you nigga," Anshon said, looking Wallo up and down, "I made your crazy lookin' ass and you can have the pussy for all the fuck I care. Fuck you, I'ma leave but don't ever in your life try and punk me nigga!" Anshon walked backwards to his car so he could leave. He didn't wanna turn his back on Wallo.

When he got in the car, he couldn't believe what had just happened. He called Monica on the phone, "You use to fuck Wallo?"

She was still half asleep, "Wha-what-what? Anshon please."

"Ain't no Anshon please. Did you fuck Wallo?"

Monica took a deep breath. "We ain't really fuck, Anshon."

"What you mean you ain't really fuck, either you did or you didn't!"

"Yes, but I was fifteen. That shit don't count."

Anshon hung up on her and drove to Fe-Fe's.

"Yo Teck," Anshon yelled, rattling Fe-Fe's front door once more.

Dragging herself to the door, Fe-Fe looked at Anshon like he was crazy, "Nigga it's 3 a.m., what is your problem?"

"Oh my fault, shawtie," Anshon, said looking away. Fe-Fe's nipples were hard and he didn't wanna take his thoughts there. "I needed to hollah at my man real quick. It's a lot of niggas gettin' held up and shit around here, Wallo is buggin', and it's just a lot of shit on my mind right now."

Fe-Fe could see the worry in Anshon's face. She let him in and locked the door behind him. "What's wrong?"

Anshon looked at Fe-Fe and he couldn't help but

see how beautiful she was, her long black hair was draped over her shoulders. "You got the kinda hair my sister has," he laughed. "My mother use to put water and lotion in it."

"That's some serious old school shit, Anshon," Fe-Fe laughed.

"I know." He stood in front of her and ran his fingers through her wavy hair. Immediately her pussy tingled. She backed away and moved slightly so his hand would fall.

"I'm buggin'," he said moving closer to her.

"I know you are," she said, allowing him to back her against the wall.

"When is Teck coming home?"

"You mean here?" she said breathing heavy, wanting desperately for him to kiss her.

"Yeah," he said licking his lips.

"He's not...I mean I don't know...we had a big argument. He said he could set his trap someplace else."

"Oh," Anshon brushed his lips across Fe-Fe's and she responded by wrapping her arms around his neck.

"Damn, I been wanting to do this for a long time," Anshon said as his hands roamed all over her ass.

"What about Monica?" Fe-Fe asked, feeling Anshon untie her sweatpants.

"She ain't here right now."

"And neither is Teck," Fe-Fe whispered.

"Can I fuck you?" Anshon said, now lifting her shirt above her head. Unsnapping her bra and freeing her breast, he took a step back.

"What?" she asked, not sure if she should be embarrassed or not.

"You are beautiful."

Before Fe-Fe could respond Anshon's cell phone started ringing. He looked at the caller I.D. and saw that it was Monica. He pressed ignore and continued to undress Fe-Fe.

"Anshon..." Fe-Fe moaned as she laid on the couch, naked and spreading her legs. "This is wrong."

"No, this is all right." He started sucking on her clit. "This feel too fuckin' good to be wrong."

Hours later Anshon and Fe-Fe had fucked every way imaginable. Anshon laid on the floor and looked at the ceiling, Fe-Fe could tell that he still had a lot on his mind.

"What's wrong, baby?" she said placing her head against his chest.

"Everything is coming down at once." Anshon turned over on his stomach and she started to rub his back. "My sister practically cussed me out because she don't want me in the game anymore, niggas is gettin' robbed all over Selma. Wallo tells me that he use to fuck Monica…and she gon' tell me it was when she was fifteen so the shit don't count. What the hell kinda shit is that?"

"Anshon," Fe-Fe took a deep breath, "Monica loves you. Don't hold that against her."

"Yeah, maybe you're right."

"I can't blame Tammy either, for wanting you out the game, even though me and Teck making mad money."

"Really?" Anshon frowned, "Teck ain't been to re-up for two weeks. I thought maybe y'all were taking it slow."

"He hasn't been to re-up?" Fe-Fe smirked, then she thought, *Maybe he really is selling in Durham.* "Maybe you should deal wit Teck on that."

121

"Oh best believe I will," Anshon said, "So Fe, what's up with all of this?" Anshon asked, turning on his side to feel on her ass again.

"Nothing," Fe-Fe unwrapped Anshon's arms from around her. "Not a thing. We can't let this happen again. As much as I wanna keep fucking you, I can't."

"Anshon sat up and reached for his clothes, "Yo' I respect that. I just thank you for being here. I felt like I was going out of my mind...oh shit." He snapped his fingers and looked at his watch, it was nine o'clock in the morning. "Tammy! Shit, I forgot that she's coming."

"She is!" Fe-Fe's face lit up, "I can't wait for her to see me clean! Maybe we can be best friends again."

"Slow down, Fe-Fe," Anshon laughed, "Go put some clothes on and then you can come with me to my house and meet her."

"Okay!" Fe-Fe said laughing on her way upstairs, "I can't wait to see her!"

Anshon ran in Fe-Fe's small bathroom downstairs and showered. As soon as he made sure his pants were straight, he saw Teck standing in the doorway, he jumped, "Damn nigga you scared the shit outta me!" Anshon held his chest.

"It's all good dawg, where Fe at?"

"Upstairs."

"Yeah."

"Yeah," Anshon said, giving Teck a pound, "I just stopped by to see if Fe-Fe wanted to ride with me to meet Tammy."

"Tammy?" Teck frowned.

"Yeah, she's coming back in town."

"Oh," Teck thought about the argument he and Fe-Fe had the other night, "Naw, she don't wanna go."

"Ai'ight," Anshon said, feeling a strange vibe from Teck. He couldn't tell if Teck felt as if something was going on with him and Fe-Fe or if Teck was just acting funny. "Fe-Fe, I'll catch you later," Anshon hollered.

Fe-Fe stood at the top of the stairs, out of Teck's sight and mouthed to Anshon, "Call me." Anshon nodded his head and then left.

"Come here, Fe-Fe," Teck ordered.

Reluctantly she walked down the stairs, "What?"

"I'm sorry about the argument we had. You forgive me?"

Fe-Fe rolled her eyes, "Niggah please. I ain't seen

123

you in a week, you've been disappearing and shit. Humph, and I don't like the way you've been acting lately. Therefore, I don't know who else you been fucking so—"

"Fe-Fe please."

"You ain't gotta lie to me, Teck. I don't give a damn."

"You know what Teck," Fe-Fe said, as if an idea had just come to her. "Get your shit and go! Don't come back. The trap is closed."

Teck really wanted to kick Fe-Fe's ass, as far as he was concerned, he'd made her. "Fuck you! Crackhead bitch!"

"Whatever," Fe-Fe huffed. "Come on so I can lock the door behind you please." After Teck left, Fe-Fe didn't even drop a tear, she cleaned up her house, took a shower, and laid down to sleep. When she woke up it was because Monica called her around two o'clock and gave her the good news that she had a job now and that she would start next week.

Fe-Fe was happy for Monica, but she felt a little sting knowing that her money was running low. Thank God for Section 8 or she would've lost her home a long time ago. Refusing to fall on her face, Fe-Fe did something she hadn't done in years, she picked up the paper and looked through the classified section. Finding an ad for a bank teller, she picked up the phone answered the add. The bank scheduled her an interview for nine o'clock the next morning.

Afterwards she picked up the phone and called her twin sons. "I wanna see you ma," Fe-Fe's son, Jason, said to her. "I miss you and I wanna get to know you, please ma?"

"Yeah, me too," said Jamal, who was on the line as well. Fe-Fe broke into tears when they asked her if she could talk to their cousin that had legal custody of them. No matter what, they wanted to be with their mother.

"Yes," Fe-Fe said, wiping tears from her eyes, "I'll be up there next week to talk with her."

As Fe-Fe hung up, and was wiping her eyes, the phone rang again. It was Monica. Fe-Fe felt guilty about fucking Anshon. She and Monica were so close, but Fe-Fe made herself be at ease, as she convinced herself that she would never sleep with Anshon again.

****

A few days later, around eight in the evening, it was a full house at Anshon's place. Anshon, Monica,

Tammy, Fe-Fe, some of the guys Anshon played ball with—Wood C, Deck, Otis, Don, Tremain—and the two sisters from next door, Dee and Plum were there. They were playing cards and listening to some old school hip-hop like MC Lyte's "Paper Thin" which was playing at the time.

Tammy was at the table with Don playing spades against Otis and Tremain.

The small card party they had going on was good for Tammy because she'd been crying non-stop since she found out that Tom-Tom was dead and her house was burnt down. When she came to Selma she wanted Anshon to take her directly to the sight of her house, but instead she changed her mind and wanted to place flowers on Tom-Tom's grave. Anshon felt like the Grim Reaper when he stepped foot on Tom-Tom's fresh soil.

He didn't sweat Tammy about the time she wanted to spend at Tom-Tom's grave. The way Anshon saw it, he felt it was better that Tammy be standing over Tom-Tom's grave, then Tom-Tom be standing over her's.

Three 40oz. bottles of Old Gold rested on Anshon's dinning room table. In the living room, Anshon sat on the floor next to Monica playing X-Box as Deck sat between Dee and Plum knocking down a 40oz. of Old Gold. Fe-Fe sat on the couch kicking it with Wood C.

"Stop cutting my damn books!" Tammy yelled at Don.

He had a drunk ass glassy look in eye. "That wheelchair got hydraulics on it?' he belched, "If not I could hook ya up. My brother is a bad motherfucker in his two wheeler!"

Normally Tammy's feelings would've been hurt, but because she knew that Don didn't mean any harm and that he was half drunk, she ignored him. "Shut the hell up and play cards." Don was so drunk that after a while Dee had to play his hand. Tammy was beatin' Dee's ass. She was running Bostons all over the place. Dee, started to get annoyed with Tammy kicking her ass, so she quit the game. "Sore loser," Tammy laughed.

Fe-Fe was bobbing her head to the music, as she peeped Don and Deck creep out behind Plum.

A few minutes later, Anshon asked, "Wood C, where the hell is Deck at?

"Wit' Plum."

Anshon could only smile, he could only imagine that they were getting ready to run a serious train. And not to be out-done, Dee somehow got Otis and Tremain to follow her next door, she said something

127

about needing a dresser moved. It was quiet with only Wood C on the couch along with Fe-Fe and Anshon changing the CDs.

Tammy looked around the room, "Damn what happen to them cats?"

Fe-Fe laughed, "They next door freakin' Plum and Dee."

Tammy shook her head. "Them girls might as well go into porn."

Don, Deck, Otis and Tremain didn't come from next door until two hours later. Wood C gave Fe-Fe his cell number then rolled out with Deck. Otis got behind the wheel of his '79 Cadillac Seville with Tremain slumped in the passenger seat and Don stretched out in the back. He blew the horn and then rolled out.

"Anshon," Fe-Fe said before she got ready to leave, "I got a job at the bank. I went for my interview yesterday and they hired me on the spot."

"Get the hell outta here!" he smiled at her.

"Yeah," she said, "My first day is tomorrow."

"That's wassup, Fe-Fe, that's wassup." Anshon kissed Fe-Fe on the cheek before she left. One good thing about Teck is that before he started acting up, he'd brought Fe-Fe a car for her to get around in.

"I'll holla at y'all in the morning. I'm going to bed," Tammy said heading for the bed.

"Good night, Big Sis."

Monica closed the bedroom door and started to undress. "I had fun tonight, baby."

"Yeah me, too. My sister's cool, right?"

"Yeah, she is," Monica said throwing her arm around him, "She really is."

****

Early the next morning Tammy was out and about. Her first mission was to stop at the bank in Raleigh to make a withdrawal to do some serious shopping. She made a withdrawal for $400.00, but a glitch in the system added an extra 0 and made it look as if she had withdrew $400,000. As soon as the teller saw the withdrawal slip, Kristi, Teck's baby mother, nearly broke her neck to call her sister, Constance.

"Constance," Kristi said, breathing heavy, "this is it, we 'bout to strike gold. This chic just made a withdrawal for 400 grand. Where's Teck and Wallo?"

"I'll call them," Constance said in a hurry.

"They better hurry before she leaves." Kristi looked out the window, "She's driving a white Mercedes truck with a handicap license plate."

"Let me call them now. Damn, Kristi, we struck gold! Maybe I can leave Selma after all."

Kristi turned around smiling and Fe-Fe was standing there. Fe-Fe couldn't believe what she just heard, she didn't know who the person was in the white Mercedes but she knew for a fact that whomever it was, that something was getting ready to go down that included this girl Kristi, and whoever she was talking to.

Kristi handed Fe-Fe the statement, "Process this," she said.

When Fe-Fe saw Tammy's name she knew something was wrong. *"Oh God, no!"* It only took a six second call to confirm that the computer made a mistake. Only 400 hundred was taken out of Tammy's account, not 400 grand. Fe-Fe walked over to Kristi's desk but she wasn't there. Fe-Fe stated to panic. She called Tammy on her cell phone but there was no answer. Then she tried Anshon and still no answer. Fe-Fe felt like she was going to have a panic attack. Her palms were sweaty and she was panting. She picked the phone back up and called Tammy's cell phone again.

"Hello?" Tammy said.

"Tammy," Fe-Fe was breathing heavy, "Please don't stop and talk—"

"Wait a minute Fe-Fe," Tammy interrupted her, "It's Te—" and the phone went dead. Fe-Fe took off running out the bank like a bat outta hell. At that point, she didn't give a damn about her job, saving Tammy was more important.

****

Anshon started to worry about his sister when 4:30 p.m. rolled around and she hadn't called. She was supposed to head back to Atlanta that morning and he knew she wanted to be on time because Q'mara, her daughter, had a school play that Tammy wouldn't dare miss.

For the last hour, Anshon had been dialing Tammy's cell phone non-stop. Then he thought to check his voicemail, maybe she called. He had two messages, the first message was from Tammy, "Hey big head, it's your Big Sis. I want you to know that I love you and that no matter what you will always be my heart. I'm heading over to the bank now to take out some money.

By the way I like Monica, but it's kinda obvious that you and Fe-Fe have a thing goin'. Are you tappin' that?" Anshon smiled, his heart felt content from hearing her voice. The message continued, "See ya when I see ya."

The second message started to play, "Anshon," Fe-Fe said breathing heavy. "Have you seen Tammy? Please get a hold to her, I think someone is trying to set her up."

Anshon felt like his heart stopped. He paced the floor back and forth for two hours. He kept calling Tammy's phone but there was no answer. The six o'clock news was just coming on. Monica nervously sat in front of the TV watching her man pace back and forth.

"Baby," she said, as the news continued, "Please come sit down. Baby—"

"Monica, be quiet," Anshon snapped, the news broadcast, caught his attention.

"This just in," the newscaster said, clearing her throat, "there was a vandalized, White Mercedes truck found in the woods of Nashville. An anonymous caller reported this to police. The police are still trying to trace where the call came in from. If you have any information on who this vehicle with North Carolina license plate EID987 belongs to please contact the authorities."

"I gotta go," Anshon said to Monica, grabbing his heat.

"Anshon!" Monica jumped, as the phone started to ring. Monica reached for the phone and snatched it off the receiver. "What!" she screamed, "You're the police? Yes, we're on the outskirts. Yes 555, Old Hudson Road, that's our address."

At the same time that Monica was giving the police the address, Fe-Fe was knocking at the door.

"Did you hear from Tammy?" She was hysterical. She took her car keys and clinched them tight, for some reason she felt as if she were holding on for dear life.

"No," Anshon said.

Fe-Fe ran into his arms and cried into his chest. He stroked her hair, "It'll be okay baby. I promise it will."

Monica was a little taken aback. She was trying to be strong for Anshon, but here he was being strong for Fe-Fe. And seeing her crying in Anshon's arms with him stroking her hair was a bit much. But then she remembered that Fe-Fe and Tammy were the best of friends. So, she swallowed what she was feeling for the moment.

When the police came, Anshon and Monica gave them all of Tammy's information and confirmed that it was her truck.

An hour after the police left, Monica looked at her watch. Shit, she was running late for work. She had already missed too many days and was in jeopardy of getting fired. She turned to Anshon, who seemed to catch the way he was holding Fe-Fe, and pushed her away. "I'ma call out of work," Monica said.

"No baby, don't. It'll be okay. Tammy will be fine," Anshon said.

Monica turned to Fe-Fe, "Don't let him out of your sight. Please. Do whatever you have to do to keep him here. And call me if something goes down." Monica grabbed her purse and headed out the door.

After Monica left, Anshon felt as if his whole body was in shock. He went into the kitchen and pulled out a bottle of gin and two 40oz.'s of Old Gold. Fe-Fe sat on the couch with tears in her eyes as Anshon sat at the table. After the gin and two 40oz.'s were gone, he stumbled to the fridge and pulled out two bottles of Mad Dog 20/20. Fe-Fe started to worry about him.

"Anshon, that's enough," Fe-Fe said standing in front of him. "Please."

He looked at Fe-Fe, pulled her close, and started kissing her. Just then, the phone rang. It was Monica.

"Hello," Fe-Fe answered the phone.

"How is he?" Monica asked.

"Drunk as hell!"

"Maybe I should come home," Monica insisted.

"No, no stay at work, everything will be okay."

Fe-Fe hung up the phone with Monica, "Let's go sit down, Anshon." She struggled to hold him up, but they fell against the sofa. He started calling out Tammy's name and crying.

"It's gonna be ok," she whispered as she wrapped her arms around him. He cried out Tammy's name again and then struggled to his feet.

"Gotta...g-go...get my sister," he slurred staggering towards the door.

"No Anshon!" she grabbed his shirt. "NO ANSHON!" she moved in front of him looking up at him.

He stopped, swayed to the side, then looked Fe-Fe dead in her eyes. "Move...I gotta get my sister."

"NO ANSHON!" she stood her ground placing one hand up on his chest. "I can't let you outta this house, boy. I can't do it, go SIT DOWN!"

"I...n-need my heat." He turned and staggered towards the bedroom.

Fe-Fe knew she couldn't let him get his gun. "ANSHON, NO!" she ran after him and caught him just as he entered the bedroom. He was heading for the closest as she tossed her body against him. The beer and wine already had his equilibrium fucked up so Fe-Fe's body on his back caused them both to tumble on the bed. Fe-Fe held him down as best she could. Every time he tried to roll out the bed, she would pull him back by the neck.

"DAMMIT ANSHON!" she said as he pushed her off causing her body to roll to the floor banging the door shut. Since the hallway light was no longer filling the room, it was now dark. Fe-Fe shot up and jumped right back on his ass as he headed for the closet once more. She grabbed the back of his pants then pulled back with all her might. When he fell back, he started crying heavily. He wrapped his arms around her. Fe-Fe knew she had to stay in his arms to keep him calm. Monica's words advising Fe-Fe to do anything to keep

Anshon in the house rung in Fe-Fe's ears as Anshon continued to cry. When he kissed her neck and moved his hands down to her waist, Fe-Fe froze up and pulled away.

"Please don't leave me," he sobbed. When he rolled over pinning Fe-Fe on her back, she tried to push him off. He lowered his mouth to hers, then kissed her. Fe-Fe couldn't believe her present situation. In bed with her best friend's man, kissing him as if he belonged to her. Anshon's hands started to roam under her shirt. He moved from her lips just as his hand reached her soft breast.

"Anshon." Tears filled her eyes as he slid her shirt up. Her lower back arched from the bed as he sloppily started to suck on her breasts. "Nooo!" she whimpered as he started to tug on her pants. Her mind was saying no, but her hips came up off the bed. She continued to cry as she felt him kiss and lick her now naked body. When she felt his tongue between her legs, she covered her face with her hands and pleaded with him to stop as she opened her legs wider.

****

Two days passed, Tammy still hadn't been found, and Anshon hadn't spoken a single word. He was sitting on the couch sucking on the tip of a Cuban cigar, thinking about how he should've packed it with hydro, as opposed to leaving the tobacco in it. Monica was leaning against his shoulders, as all of Anshon's boys, with the exception of Teck and Wallo, sat around the living room, waiting to see what their next move should be.

Breaking the silence was a rattling at the screen door. Anshon jumped up and two detectives were standing there. Anshon invited the detectives in and everybody stood up, wanting desperately to hear the words that Tammy had been found alive.

Wood C and Deck lowered their heads as one of the detectives started to speak. "Mr. Green, I'm sorry to have to tell you this, but we were able to identify a body found by Neuse River, near Dunn, as being your sister, Tammy." Wood C pulled his glasses off and tears rolled down his face. Anshon stood silent. He was in shock. The detective continued, "Her body was dismembered, naked, and mutilated, we were able to identify it as being her by her dental records." Anshon stared at the detectives. His eyes rolled to the back of his head and he passed out.

Monica fell to the floor and cradled his head trying to revive him. "Come on baby. Please, come on."

Slowly, Anshon started to open his eyes, "Why she die, Fe, why?"

Monica wiped his tears, she was too hurt behind Tammy's death and Anshon's reaction to worry about how he'd just called her Fe-Fe's name.

The next day Tammy's two children and Aunt Rosa, who they were all living with, flew into town. They'd caught the first plane to RDU when Anshon had called to tell them. Aunt Rosa went along with Monica to identify Tammy's body. Anshon couldn't do it. There wasn't a wake held for Tammy due to the condition of her body and the funeral, held at Howell's Chapel in Selma, was a closed casket.

While the day was bright, Anshon's life was bland and colorless. For his sister, he led a 75-car procession over every inch of asphalt in Smithfield and Selma in his '77 Chevy with the top down as Jay-Z's instrumental version of "Song Cry" played loudly. Anshon drove slowly with the hazard lights on, the system on blast, and the song locked on repeat. In his mind, he was taking his sister on her last ride. When they rolled through Selma down Preston street, folks stood on the curb waving or crying . Kenny-Mac's 30 deep bike club was acting as the traffic stoppers and Selma's finest had sense enough to sit their ass on the sideline and be easy. Niggas were grieving for somebody that didn't need to die. When Tammy's casket was lowered into the ground, Anshon closed his eyes and for the first time since he was a child, he said a prayer. "Now I lay me down to sleep, I pray to the Lord my soul to keep. If I should die before I wake, I pray to the Lord my soul to take." It was the prayer that Tammy taught him when he was five. She told him that it would fight off the devil.

Anshon pounded his chest, so that it wouldn't collapse. He held his nephew, Q'shon's hand, who was holding Q'mara's hand, and he said to them, "Uncle Anshon got you. Don't even worry about it."

Anshon's pain was beyond a broken heart and tears. At this moment, he knew that a part of him was dead and there would be no turning back. He couldn't seem to shake Tammy's conversation with him when he begged her to let him deeper into the game. He thought about how she told him, "You can handle your enemies, but you need God to help you with your friends." At that moment, it clicked. Teck and Wallo had to have their wig split. Anshon didn't know how or why they killed Tammy. But something in his heart told him that they had done it...and now, it was their time to pay. Fuck forgiveness, fuck letting it slide, someone else besides Tammy had to die.

To Anshon the world was nothing without his sister. She was his everything.

Chapter 8

Eleven days had passed since Tammy was buried. Everybody else, but Anshon was getting on with their life. Teck and Wallo were no where to be found, but Anshon had his hit out.

Fe-Fe continued to work at the bank, because Anshon asked her too. He felt she could find out where Teck and Wallo were and how her co-worker, Kristi, was involved.

"Anshon, get the door," Monica yelled from the kitchen. She was baking a cake and there was a knock at the front door.

"Wassup?" Anshon said, giving Deck a pound.

"Nuthin'. Wanted to know if you wanna shoot some ball today?"

"Naw, not today, kinda hot." Deck gave him another pound before he turned to leave.

"Anshon, let's go see Q'mara and Q'shon," Monica said, shifting through the eleven days worth of mail that laid on the kitchen table. "Bills..." she mumbled to herself, "mo' bills...mo' bills...Triple Crown...another bill. Wait a minute, Triple Crown?" She called Anshon to come where she was. He stood in the kitchen doorway sipping on a cold one. "Baby, ain't Triple Crown a publishing company?"

Anshon frowned, "Hell yeah they're a publishing company. Shit, they write about the shit we live. Tammy use to read their books all the time."

"Well," Monica said holding the letter up, "they sent her a letter."

Anshon's face lit up. "Big Sis was writing a book," Anshon laughed. "She practically cussed my ass out because I laughed when she told me. Oh shit, give me the letter." Monica handed him the letter and he ripped it open. He read it and looked at Monica, "Baby, they offered Tammy a book deal! They wanna publish her book!"

"Alright baby! Alright!" Monica yelled. "See Anshon, she'll live on. She will."

Anshon called Triple Crown and spoke on behalf of his departed sister. They expressed their sympathy and were happy to be the ones to help keep Tammy's memory alive. And for the first time since Tammy died, Anshon was able to smile.

He stood outside on his patio and tipped his 40oz. over the ledge. "This one's for you Big Sis. *Hood Legend* is gonna be on the street's after all."

Monica went to grab the phone, to call and tell his Aunt Rosa the good news. As she picked it up, a woman was already on the line.

"Ah yes, may I speak to Anshon Green?"

"Who is dis!" Monica asked wondering who in the hell this woman was calling her man. She looked at the phone and the caller I.D. was marked private. *Oh hell naw! Fe-Fe is one thing but another bitch? Oh hell no!* she thought.

"I'm not at the liberty to say that," the woman said.

"Look BITCH!" Monica stood up. "Don't be fuckin' callin' my man 'cause-"

"Gimme the phone!" Anshon held out his hand. "Yo, who dis?"

"Anshon, we need to talk."

Monica ran to the backroom to pick up the phone. It wasn't Fe-Fe so Anshon didn't care about her picking up the line, as a matter of fact he didn't start talking until he could hear Monica breathing on the phone. "I'll talk when I find out who the hell this is!"

"You may not remember me, but this is Larrisha Maynard, we use to date in high school."

"High school? Larrisha Maynard? Don't even play yaself home girl. Sorry I stood you up for the prom, but goddamn you should be over it by now. So, Larrisha, I don't know how you got this number, but I'ma kindly ask you not to call here no more."

"Damn straight!" Monica added. "Stank pussy bitch!"

"You the stank pussy bitch, hoe!" Larrisha snapped, "And Anshon, don't flatter yourself. I'm calling because I work here at the bank with Fe-Fe and she was too upset to tell you what we found out today, so I'm calling to fill you in."

"Speak," Anshon said. Monica was silent.

"I need to talk to you face to face."

"Larrisha—"

"I know who killed your sister." She cut him off.

"I'll meet you at the Burger King on New Bern Avenue at eight. I drive a blue Porsche."

"YO, WHAT THE FUCK!" he yelled, but she had already hung up. When he called Fe-Fe's she was crying so bad that he couldn't understand a word she was saying.

"What's going on?" Monica asked, following Anshon around the house. He went into the living room to search through the phone book for the number to the bank. He tossed the phone on the couch when he was informed that Larrisha Maynard no longer worked at the bank. His temper continued to rise. *So she lied, she just told me that she worked at the bank with Fe-Fe. What the fuck is going on?*

"Let's call the police," Monica said softly.

"Hell no!"

"Baby, please don't go see her. What if she's trying to set you up or something?" she pleaded with him.

Anshon wasn't hearing a word Monica was saying. As far as Anshon was concerned, Biggie said it best, "kick in the door waving the four-four." Scratch that and fuck a .44. Anshon had a gorilla under the bed. A gold plated 4 $\frac{1}{2}$ pound, 8 $\frac{1}{2}$ inch barrel, five shot Smith & Wesson .50 caliber Magnum revolver.

"Monica, listen to me." He turned her face towards him, pointing to the gun. Monica jumped to the floor. Anshon looked at the gun in his hand and laid it on the bed. "My fault, baby...but listen Princess, I swear I'm not losing nobody else that's close to me. My Momma gone, my sister gone, I never knew my coward ass Daddy...you all a nigga got." Fe-Fe crossed his mind, but he didn't call out her name. "Baby, if the wind fuckin' blow hard, I'ma stand in front of you. Don't try to change my mind on this. But if I ever...ever find out who took my Big Sis away from me, I'ma kill 'em." Anshon picked up his cell and called Wood C and Deck. They agreed to go with him. Anshon turned to Monica, "I'm leaving."

Monica knew there was nothing she could do. "Please be careful Baby."

"I will. I'm pickin' up Wood C and Deck on my way and I'll call you as soon as I get there."

She threw a kiss at him through the window, then stood in the front yard to watch him leave.

Since the sun was setting, it was a little dusky as the street lights slowly came on. Monica wiped her eyes then went to lock the door. A few seconds later she pulled out in her Nissan.

50 Cent's "I'm Suppose To Die Tonight" filled

Anshon's cruising Chevy as he headed towards Raleigh. Anshon made sure he drove the posted speed limit because right now was not a good time to be handing out his license and registration to the police...not with his gorilla sitting heavily in his lap. Wood C was sitting in the front passenger seat, smoking a big head with two Glock .40's under his arms in leather holsters as Deck sat quietly in the back with a pistol grip 32-round clip U.S. Ingram MAC-11.

"Niggas think this is game," Anshon shouted pulling into Burger King's parking lot. "They think I'm fuckin' playin'."

Wood C took a pull off his big head, "Niggas think they goin' home but they're not."

"'Cause they gon be sittin' up in the trunk startin' to rot," Anshon rapped a little.

Anshon's backed into a dark parking spot. It was dark outside, so as Anshon cut the head lights off his car faded into the night.

"I'ma go in and order sumthin?" Wood C pulled out his twin .40. "These clowns might call the police thinkin' we plottin' to rob the joint."

"Nah," Anshon said, "I'ma go in, just in case she's inside but drove another whip 'cause I don't see no blue Porsche."

Just as Anshon went to pull the latch on the door a stunning Carolina blue Audi A8L pulled up and stopped in front of Anshon's Chevy. When the tinted window slid down, Deck simultaneously raised the MAC-11 hoping and praying that whoever was in the Audi tripped.

Wood C and Anshon pressed their bodies against the door in case Deck made up his mind to bust off through the front windshield.

"It's a bitch," Deck said, slowly lowering the MAC-11. Anshon rose up and saw Larrisha sitting behind the wheel. She had changed a little over the years but for the most part, she still looked the same. He picked up his 4 $\frac{1}{2}$ pound .50 and got out. It was hard as hell to hide the gorilla in his pants. Fuck it

"Where dey at? And how the fuck you know about my sister?" Anshon fired his questions before Larrisha could even get all the way out of the car.

"Anshon…we have to sit down and I'll tell you all this from the start. I know you are upset, but please," she said slightly above a whisper.

"YO, YOU DON'T WANT IT WIT ME KID, FOR REAL YOU DON'T." He was tempted to pull that gold .50. Larrisha remained calm. Anshon heard a car pulling up so he stepped closer to Larrisha, never taking his eyes off her.

"Please Anshon, follow me back to my house."

"Where's Fe-Fe?" Anshon asked, "I thought you said she knew."

"She does, but she doesn't know everything."

His gut instinct told him not to go, but he needed to find out what Larrisha knew about his sister's death.

Anshon rode with Larrisha to her house while Wood C and Deck following behind in his car. Once inside, Larrisha asked if anyone wanted anything to drink, they all declined. Larrisha sat down and looked at Anshon.

"So what's up? I ain't come here to flirt," Anshon said sarcastically.

Larrisha crossed her legs, clearing her throat. "I'll start from the very beginning. You already know that I work at the bank or I used to. Fe-Fe caught the tail end of everything going on, but I was there from the beginning. There's a teller at the bank who I believe is tied up in your sister's murder."

"Who, how and why?" Anshon asked.

"Please let me explain. Your sister made a $400 withdrawal, but a glitch in the system said it was 400 grand. Fe-Fe checked the account and saw that it was wrong. When she left that day in a panic, she dropped the bank slip. I picked it up and checked the account behind her."

"And?" Anshon said, wanting her to hurry up and get to the point. "Fuck all that. Who the fuck killed my Big Sis?"

Larrisha sighed, uncrossing her legs. "See, I started to notice how after every big withdrawal being made that the teller, Kristi, would leave. And the next day somebody would end up robbed, shot, or found dead. Well, the day that Tammy came into the bank, Kristi made up a lie about her daughter being sick and needing to leave…I know I should not have, but I followed her. First, she went to the Crabtree Valley Mall. I thought I was wasting my time until I saw Kristi park and get into a white Mercedes truck. That's when I started paying close attention. Forty minutes went by and then she pulled out. I was right behind her and she never noticed me.

Five minutes after she pulled out of the parking lot, I noticed that Kristi was making the same turn that a motorcycle was making.

"She was driving my sister's truck." Anshon swallowed hard. His blood pressure was starting to rise. Deck and Wood C remained silent.

"I stayed on Kristi's tail," Larrisha continued, "but I lost her on a back road in Nashville. As I sat waiting for the light to turn green, I noticed her cross back over the street and turn down a dirt road. When the light changed, I followed the skid marks. The same guy that was on the motorcycle was waiting there for Kristi. Then Kristi dumped the truck, hopped on the back of the bike; they looked around, and then took off. When I pulled along side of the truck, I saw the car registration and driver's license on the front seat. That's when I saw that it was your sister, Tammy, so I called the police with an anonymous tip."

"So it's that bitch Kristi? I'ma kill her! And the bike…that's Wallo. I swear to God they're done!" Anshon felt like breaking down crying, but he was determined to hold it together.

"What the fuck you trying to do?" Larrisha snapped, "Go to jail? Just chill for a minute. You can't always show your hand."

Anshon shot her a look the last time he heard that, it was when Wallo said it. "Go on and finish," he said.

Larrisha took a deep breath, "I don't think it's just

Kristi. I believe I know who else is involved, but I need to be sure before I give you a name."

"Why the hell are you telling me all of this?" Anshon clinched his jaw, "Why the hell you ain't tell the police?"

Larrisha looked dead into his eyes. "I have a brother, Anshon. My brother, Von was in the pool hall that night with Doughnut's baby mother. Doughnut could have killed my brother...so I know if I was in your shoes...let's say this. Don't let my feminine looks fool you. I'll kill for my brother and still put my lip gloss on straight."

Anshon's eyes started to fill up with tears. Larrisha knew that his pain was hurting him deep. She felt like crying herself. Anshon realized that his sister was tortured for money she didn't have. Tears rolled down his face. His vision blurred as Deck and Wood C stood there trying not to cry.

"Yo," Wood C spoke for the first time. "How you livin' so large? I know these cribs out here cost 'bout three hundred G's or bettah. And my man said you had a Boxter and now you pushin' an Audi, your clown ass brother ridin' in a Volvo with spinners. How we know you ain't followin' peeps and doin' your thang, answer that?"

Anshon wiped his eyes then glared at Larrisha. Wood C was dead on the money. Larrisha ignored the remark about her brother as she reached for her Marc Jacobs tote bag from the floor. She opened it then pulled out a business card then handed it to Wood C.

L&K
Investment Consultants

We Research, Observe, Borrow
&
Keep Investments Limited & Legit

Ms. L. Maynard
&
Ms. K. Batts
(919) 827-1975

Larrisha allowed him a few seconds to study the card before she explained the legal hustle she ran with her brother. Wood C looked up.

"We research the stock market, New York Stock Exchange," Larrisha continued, "the Amex and Nasdaq to find the hot commodities or a company that will soon be in a real high demand. We then observe the buying trend of that market and if it looks good, we borrow money to buy shares or make an investment. Our motto is, 'We keep investments limited, that way we never take a big loss if things flop and of course," she smiled, "we keep all our business legit."

Larrisha pulled the diamond pin from her hair then explained to Anshon how she had a plan that she felt would work…a plan that her brother didn't agree with, but she didn't care. Anshon was all ears, but all he wanted was a name; but for now, he'd play her game.

Anshon, Wood C and Deck made it back to Selma before twelve that night. Monica was in the bed asleep, but quickly woke up. "Anshon, baby, what's going on?"

He gave her the short version, leaving out some details on purpose. Then he took off his clothes, showered and changed. "Deck and Wood C in the living room waiting on me," he said before leaving again,

"We gon' run by Ms. Johnnie Ray's shot house. I promise I'll be back by 3:00 a.m."

Monica didn't really want him to go but she felt that she had no choice, "Okay baby."

Anshon took the backseat in Wood C's 300C as they headed to get their drink on. When they pulled up, they found the spot packed. The twins saw Wood C's 300C and waved him over to park behind their chromed out minivans.

"Sup Dawg? E'rythang straight?" Teck said giving them some dap. Wallo followed his brother's lead.

"Look Anshon," Wallo said, "I know we had some words the other day, but it's all good we still peoples and shit. I'm sorry to hear about Tammy. I just found out. I was down in Murfreesboro, my aunt died."

Anshon nodded his head to make them think that everything was straight.

"Ai'ight," Teck said, "First round on me."

"Y'all just gettin' here?" Anshon asked going up the stone steps.

"Yeah. Fid'na get tipsy then find sumthin' to smash," Teck replied.

Once inside the 1930's built house, the music was blasting and a thick haze of smoke filled the living room. Big titty Gale was solo dancing on the worn out carpet with a glass of gin in one hand a cup of O.J. in the other. Al Green's music was helping her to get her groove on.

In the kitchen, two old heads were beefing at each other over a domino game while Fernistein stood at the gas stove frying chicken. Teck and Wallo had stopped cooking food in the yard, so Ms. Johnnie Ray started selling food again. Staying true to his word, Teck pulled out his knot and hit Freddy off to pay for the first rounds of brew. Freddy ran the liquor spot with Ms. Johnnie Ray along with a short temper and an even shorter sawed-off pistol grip pump. On the low…this spot was a brothel so Freddy and Ms. Johnnie Ray could also be held liable as pimps. They had two Mexicans from Smithfield that were far from attractive, but that was ok, because it was pussy they were selling. The taller one with the black hair signaled Wallo out and talked him into following her to the back. Teck shook his head then turned to the Anshon, Wood C, and Deck.

"Why you in such a good mood?" Anshon shouted to Teck over Al Green playing in the background.

"You ain't heard?" Teck moved in closer. "I beat the McMillan basketball team today!"

"Yeah right," Wood C replied leaning on the freezer.

"Word daw," Teck proclaimed.

"Who was all out there?" Anshon asked finding it hard to believe.

Teck held a finger up as he downed his cup of gin. "Whew!" he pounded his chest, as the gin caused a burning sensation in his chest. "Shit like moonshine! But anyway, Markie was out there…Clevan, Kayo, Varis, Fonz and his brother and some herbs from Micro."

"What was the score?" Anshon asked before he sipped his gin and juice.

"We won by one, twenty-one to twenty," Teck bragged. He then went on to tell them about Janis out in Johnston Court in Smithfield. How she having a welcome home party for her sister who had pulled a five year bid. They all wondered who would be the lucky man to bust that pussy wide open. Deck, finished with the Latin whore in the back, excused himself to go make a call. He dipped out to the front yard to use his cell phone and called Don. His 14-year old sister, Fatima, picked up on the sixth ring.

"Who dis?" Fatima asked.

"Don in?" Deck asked.

"Nope."

"Where he at?"

"I 'on't know. He left on a motorcycle about an hour ago."

"Who bike he on?"

"'On't know, boy. Ain't keepin' tabs on him."

"Ai'ight. Just tell 'im to call me and to bring my clippers next time he come by my crib."

"Okay, bald head," she giggled before she hung up.

Deck flipped his phone closed then headed back inside. In the corner, he saw Anshon and Teck in a deep conversation. Wood C was tripping out with Gale, dancing and sipping on gin. Every new song that came on she would raise an arm in the air and shout, "Dats my shit!"

The scene kinda took Deck back to the good old days. Club 82 back in 1994...man he missed those days. If there was beef, it was settled with the hands, but now it was all about the chrome or metal. He went up to Freddy and bought a cup of gin with no chaser, then posted up against the freezer to watch Wood C get his clown on.

Anshon moved from the corner to sit on a stool as Teck went to take a piss. He yelled out for Freddy to fill him one up with a squirt of juice. He spun around on the stool to come face to face with the second Mexican chick.

"You wanna go talk?" she said with a slight accent.

"Nah, I'm good Senorita," he said turning her down.

"Are you sure? I bet I can suck your dick all the way down my throat."

"No haps on this one."

She said something under her breath in Spanish then stepped off. Freddy handed him his drink a few seconds later. This would be his last round. He later joined Wood C, Teck and some dude from Kenly at the dominos table. He was feeling good as hell. Wallo was getting his major trick action on with the Mexican. First he had her snort a line of powder off the length of his erect dick, then had her suck him off. He got souped up then rolled on a jimmy and fucked her doggy style in the back bedroom. He spanked her and told her to call him Daddy. After he paid for her services, he went to the bathroom and walked in on Big Titty Gale.

"Boy!" she shouted. "You see me in here. Get tha fuck out!"

Deck was done with the gin, it was time to get his smoke on. Oh yeah, Freddy, also sold some phat joints and the weed was straight! Freddy stayed busy as Deck asked him for some hot sauce for his chicken. "A nigga feeling good tonight," he joked.

About six or seven minutes later, Wallo exited the bathroom. Taking a large bite from his greasy chicken, Deck went to empty his bladder. From across the room Teck yelled out that he was on his last domino. Deck staggered into the bathroom and kicked the door closed behind him. He was halfway finished pissing when he heard someone cough behind him. He nearly pissed on his jeans as he reached for his .32. The cough came from behind the dingy shower curtain. Deck opened it with the stubby barrel of his .32. only to find Gale curled up in the tub with a bloody mouth. Deck used to kick it with her niece back in the days and Gale had once hid him in the closet when his P.O. was looking for him. So, he felt close to her. He put up his .32 then reached down to help Gale out of the tub. "What the hell you doin', Gale?"

"One of dem twins tried to make me suck his dick," she murmured.

"Say what!"

"Don't cause no trouble, Deck," she pleaded as Deck helped her stand up.

"Did he hit you?"

"Yeah...but it ain't nothing. I'ma be fine."

"Look," Deck said reaching for a towel. "Clean yourself up and go home."

She pushed the towel away with a frown on her face. "Get dat nasty thing outta my face. Dem Mexicans might be using dat to wipe their funky tails."

Deck saw that she was fine, just had a small cut on her lip. Leaving her, he went back into the living room to find Anshon, Wood C and Teck getting up from the domino table. He searched for Wallo and found him standing by the door feeling up on the second Mexican. Deck approached the group just as Teck was telling Anshon and Wood C that they should roll with them to Johnston Court. Wallo walked over to his brother's side. Deck was waiting for an opening in the conversation, then played his part.

"Y'all hear about Robert?" Deck asked the group.

"Nah, whut up?" Teck asked.

"Man, that lame ass coward got locked up for beatin' on his girl. Said he broke her arm or some shit."

"Word?" Anshon replied.

"Yeah," Deck continued with his eyes locked on Wallo. "To me, a nigga is a straight bitch if he hits a woman."

"Fuck you mean muggin' me fo'?" Wallo said returning Deck's glare.

"Cause you'se a lame ass nigga. That's why!"

"Hold up, Deck!" Anshon put his hand on Deck's chest. He looked at Deck like he was crazy. Hell, he was fuckin' up the plan they had.

"Yeah, hold up nigga!" Teck jumped in. "You got beef with my brother?"

"Fuck you and your coward bitch ass brother, nigga!" Deck snapped.

"Say what!" Teck reached under his Zoo York shirt. Wallo did the same but they were slow to the punch as Wood C had his two 40's aimed at their chest.

"What the fuck?" Anshon shouted as he tried to calm things down. "Deck what's up?"

Wood C kept his two pistols aimed at the twins, while Deck told Anshon what Big Gale had just laid on him. Anshon nodded his head. "Wood C put the heat up." He turned to Teck and Wallo, "Y'all need to roll out...I'll call you tomorrow Teck." Anshon said as the twins walked towards their new Nissan minivans.

"Yeah dawg," Teck shouted over his shoulder. "And you bettah let Deck and Wood C know wassup. We got guns too. I'ma let this shit ride. But a nigga come at me or my brother sideways again ain't gonna be no talkin'. Nigga bettah keep ya third eye peeled open."

"Don't be makin' no threats on my fam," Anshon warned him.

Teck sucked his teeth. "Fuck you! You better be easy nigga, cause you could get it too. Matter a fact, fuck all you bitches, y'all can suck my dick!"

"You gotta lot of mouth," Anshon snapped.

"You don't put fear in my heart. Nigga you must got me mixed up with Tom-Tom."

"Let it go, Teck," Anshon said.

"Come to Durham and get put to sleep cowards. You bettah recognize."

"Teck!" Wallo called out to his brother. "Fuck all

this lip boxin' let's roll on them niggahs. They know where we live at, fuck 'em."

As the twins drove off, Wood C moved beside Anshon and Deck.

"You know we got beef with them clowns," Wood C said, pulling out a Newport. "What was that Tom-Tom remark about?" Wood C asked.

Anshon played it off by shrugging his shoulders. "Check this," Anshon said, "Them clowns even bend a blade of grass in my yard...I'll kill 'em. Yo take me home, I'm done for tonight."

****

Early the next morning, Constance was at the Super 8 Motel in Smithfield with Wallo. She was on her elbows and knees as he drilled her from the back. Sweat coated her naked body as their moans filled the dark room. Her ass was jiggling like jelly as his hips smacked into her ass over and over. She clutched the pillow in her hands as her pussy started to tingle. She loved to get fucked this way.

"Harder!" she shouted over her shoulder then threw her left hand back to place it on his sweaty stomach. She felt him grip her waist tighter, pulling her back against his strokes. She arched her ass higher in the air and started breathing through her mouth. "I'm gonna cummmm!" she moaned.

At the same time in the room next door, Kristi sat on the bed beside Teck watching TV. It was the first time she'd seen him since Tammy's murder.

"What's wrong wit you?" Teck asked.

"Nothing," she mumbled. "Just had a long day that's all."

"Yeah right," he frowned. "You still think we holdin' out on the money huh? I told you she didn't have shit on her."

"Look," she looked at him. " I saw the bank statement myself! I know she had the money…but she didn't have to die for it. Did you let her see your face or something?"

"Yeah and she saw my tattoo. Plus she called my name and accused me of shooting her the first time."

"Well you did!"

"So the fuck what! That's why I had to do her in this time. I know she would've told."

"Goddamn Teck!" Kristi screamed, "We made a deal that nobody would get killed, that's what the masks are for. Goddamn, first the robbery in the club that night got fucked up by Doughnut and now this!"

"Fuck all that," Teck said. "We wouldn't be so behind if you hadn't fucked up most of the $287,000 we robbed Tammy of from the first heist!"

Kristi rolled her eyes. "That still isn't an excuse to kill."

"Like you got a damn conscience now. You driving a Lex with blood money."

"This is a bunch of crap," she huffed.

"Whatchu say!"

"Nothing. Just drop the issue."

He switched the TV off and told her to shut up and undress. Reluctantly she did as he asked.

Back in Constance's room, she was having the same conversation with Wallo. And she too, wanted to know why they had killed Tammy. She just couldn't understand it, especially after the way shit backfired with Doughnut. Plus she didn't receive her usual cut and was tired of all this robbing with nothing to show for it. Sure, she had a new Benz, but she was still struggling to make ends meet.

At first things were okay but then they started to get out of hand. Now she felt like they were robbing for anything. Now they were making licks for something as petty as five grand. Constance was starting to get a bad feeling about the entire set up. Sure, she loved Wallo and had a baby with him, but she would quickly draw the line when it came to going to prison because of him. Ride or die was not on her mind. She knew how Anshon felt about his sister and she had lost a lot of respect for her man behind Tammy's death. Kristi was now afraid of Teck and her building fear pushed her towards betrayal. She loved him, but not that much. She agreed with anything he said to avoid beef. She was relieved when he got tired of her attitude and left.

She got out of bed and went to her sister's room. Wallo had just left out on his motorcycle. So now, Kristi and Constance were alone and scared. They quickly devised a plan to make sure they wouldn't go down when the shit hit the fan.

****

Monica surprised Anshon when he got home. He was in the bathroom brushing his teeth when she came in with her birth control pills in her hand. He watched her flush them down the toilet.

"Anshon, I want a baby," she said with tears in her eyes.

It was a subject they had already spoken on and Anshon was with it. They made love in the bathroom then moved to their bedroom. Each stroke he told her how much he loved her and that she was the only woman for him. And although he had to keep pushing thoughts of Fe-Fe out of his mind, he was serious about what he told Monica. Her nails had dug into his waist as she clung to him. Monica was madly in love with Anshon and would do anything for him and was whole-heartedly committed to him.

Earlier when Anshon was in Raleigh with Wood C and Deck, she drove to a gun shop in Benson and bought a pump that was now under the bed. She'd kill for her man and when he planted his seed deep inside her, she cried out his name while her pussy exploded with pleasure.

****

Fe-Fe slid out of bed trying to shake thoughts of Anshon from her mind. She tipped down the hall, and peeked into the bedroom she'd fixed up for her sons. Her cousin agreed to let them come and stay with her for a while. Fe-Fe couldn't wait. As she walked on the cold floor, she felt a chill go up her spine. She'd been sick for a little over a week now and her breast had been sore for a while. She reached in her bathroom cabinet and pulled out a pregnancy test kit she had purchased at Wal-Mart, this was actually the second test she'd brought this week. The first test she took, she swore the results were wrong. So being that she was feeling better, she thought she'd try it again. She pissed on the tab then waited for the sign.

"Damn!" she muttered a few minutes later, it was just like the first one. "Fendisha Lloyd," she said to herself, "how the hell did you let this happen?" Right away, there was no question of who the child's father was, the only problem would be telling him.

Chapter 9

Anshon woke up with a lot on his mind. He was thinking about Larrisha and if she could really lead him to the muthafuckers that took his sister's life. He had no doubt in his mind that he would kill again. But he had to control his temper or else Monica would be paying him visits in the Central Prison. And that was not what he wanted.

He remained still about an hour and then slowly he slid the covers down Monica's waist until her soft, bodacious brown ass was fully exposed. He licked his fingers, then raised his hand, then brought it down hard. Monica woke up screaming and rubbing her stinging butt cheek as Anshon rolled out of bed before she could retaliate.

"BOY!" she shouted. "That shit hurt. I'ma get your

ass!" she kicked the covers off and jumped out of the bed. Tits and ass bouncing everywhere, and it was a lovely sight to see. Since he had a head start on her, he was able to slam and lock the bathroom door in her face.

"BE OUT IN A SEC!" he shouted through the door laughing as she pounded on the door. "Dat ass hot ain't it?" he laughed.

"You can't stay in there all day!"

"Yeah, yeah, yeah, I'll holla at ya later, Princess." He flipped the lid on the toilet and took a long relaxing piss that made him tingle and twitch at the end.

"Open the door," she pleaded. "I gotta pee."

"Hol' up shawtie."

"For real! I gotta pee real bad!" she pleaded.

"If I let you in…can I look?" he asked.

"Look at what?"

"Look at you pee?"

"Boy, I don't care."

"Ai'ight, but don't cut one loose up in here," he laughed. He was still butt ass naked when he unlocked the door and opened it. And there stood his thick ass girl, naked with a smile on her face and a plastic 40oz. cup of ice cold water.

"AAGGGGGHHH!!" Anshon yelled as Monica doused his ass. He cringed as the cold water shocked him from head to toe. "That shit was cold!" he said, through clenched teeth. Monica burst out with laughter as the empty cup fell from her hands. She was still laughing as she pushed pass him to take a piss after flipping the seat back.

"We even now?" Monica said as she finished using the bathroom.

"Yeah," he said rubbing his ass. "I'm jumpin' in the shower."

Monica waited til he closed the curtain and turned the water on before she flushed the toilet. "Slide over, Bookie," she said joining him in the shower. They took turns cleaning each other from head to toe.

"French toast or pancakes?" she asked ringing her rag out as Anshon stood under the shower. She liked to look at his naked muscular body that turned her on with ease and took care of her needs 24/7.

"Pancakes," he said wiping water from his eyes.

"Umm...bacon or sausage?"

"Both."

"Boy, make-up your mind!" she said popping his ass with the rag. She reached out and rubbed the spot before he could do it himself. "That better?"

"Yes," he nodded, still wiping water from his face. "I'll take bacon." He made his mind up. She already knew the rest—scrambled cheese eggs, grits with breakfast sausage from the can and toast. "Monica." His body glistened from the creamy baby oil Monica had rubbed on him as they stood in the middle of the bathroom.

"Um, what?"

"I love you," he said caressing her oily breasts.

"I love you more, Bookie."

As they ate breakfast the temperature outside was creeping up to 89°.

"What's up for today?" Monica asked lounging on the sofa in a pair of Triple S High School gym shorts and a tank top.

"We can work on the baby all day," he said crunching on his piece of bacon.

"Now that sounds like a good idea. But I'm on top

first." Monica laughed as the phone rang. She reached across him, picked it up, and handed it directly to Anshon. It was Wood C.

"Holla."

"Yo," Wood C said. "I ran into the twins at the Waffle House last night."

"What happened?" Anshon moved to the sofa.

"Teck was there and he wanted to shake on the beef. He wanted it squashed."

"Word?" Anshon was surprised because Teck wasn't known to cop a plea.

"Yeah. We went to check on Lori's party. He told me to call you and try to let the shit die. He said y'all go way back and that Wallo was in the wrong, you know how shit be."

"What about Deck?"

"Called him over the phone."

"Good. That's less stress I gotta worry about."

"I feel ya. But yo," Wood C said, "let me know the deal 'bout what ole girl, Larrisha say. You know I'm wit'cha on layin' down whoever-"

"Yeah, I got cha," Anshon said cutting him off. The thought of Tammy made him wanna cry. "Biggie said it best," he added.

"Somebody gots ta die!" they said simultaneously.

"Anshon," Monica said when she saw him press the end button on the phone.

"Yeah?"

"Would you...really kill somebody?"

Anshon laid the phone on the table. "Don't ask me nothing like that Princess."

She lowered her head. "I wish none of this had happened. What if something go wrong and you end up in prison?"

"Princess-"

"Wait," she looked at him. "What about me, Anshon? I know you loved your sister...but we both know how she felt about you going back to prison. That night we went out to get some beer, she was telling me to not let you stay in the game."

"Monica have I been selling anything since Tammy died?"

"No."

"Ai'ight then, case closed."

She reached out to touch his shoulder. "Baby I don't wanna see you go to prison."

"Shut the fuck up!" he exploded. "SHE WASN'T YOUR GODDAMN SISTER!" Before Monica could calm Anshon down, he had threw on his clothes, snatched his keys off the table, and headed for the door.

"Anshon, wait. ANSHON, WAIT!" Monica shouted running to the door. When she grabbed his shirt, he turned and twisted from her grip. "Baby, please don't leave!" Tears filled her eyes as she stood on the porch watching him get into his car. "ANSHON!" she pleaded, as he rolled out the driveway.

****

Anshon didn't make it back home until 9:30 p.m. He'd been riding around for hours. He felt bad leaving Monica the way he had and knew he needed to go back home and apologize.

As soon as he opened the door, he paused at the sight of countless burning candles. All of the furniture was moved into the kitchen. He closed the door. When his eyes adjusted to the dim lit setting, he saw several pillows and silk sheets in the middle of the floor. Just as he was about to call Monica's name, Kem's "Love Calls" came from the back room followed seconds later by Monica appearing in the hallway. Anshon was speechless as she walked towards him. Her skin was glowing with oil and her sexy brown body was covered with a purple J-Lo lace thong and a sheer matching corset. Her cleavage was big enough to catch and seduce Anshon's eyes with ease. On her feet were a pair of purple stilettos. His hard dick beat his mouth to the apology he owed her.

"Shhhh." She started to undress him. "Don't you ever in your life leave me again, Anshon." She pulled his shirt off and made him step out of his pants. "Tonight, we ain't gonna do no talking. I'ma show and prove my love, not lust, but love for you." She pulled him to the floor and let nature take it's course.

****

Fe-Fe was surprised when Teck showed up at her front door. She hadn't seen him since last month nor had she wasted her time in calling his ass. She was home alone dressed in nothing, but her Champion t-shirt.

"What's up?" she asked letting him in.

"Just thought I'd swing by to see how you doin'," he

said looking at her bare legs. He knew she probably sported some panties under that shirt. "Got company?" he asked.

"Fool, you think I'd let your ass in if I had company?"

"Shit, you walking around in your t-shirt with no panties on." He grinned, flipping the hem of her shirt up.

"Cause it's my damn house! Even if it is a fifty-dollar a month section eight spot. The shit is mine! " she flicked the lights on. "What happened to your tattoo. The eagle on your shoulder?" She pointed to his bare arms, he was wearing a wife beater.

"I had it removed." She looked at him again and for a moment, she could've sworn that he was Wallo. Wallo and Teck may have been identical twins, but most people could tell them a part by the way they acted, but right at this moment, Fe-Fe didn't know the difference.

"Damn...why you lookin' at me all crooked?" he asked.

"Do you see what time it is?" she folded her arms.

He glanced at his watch. "It's 11:15 p.m. Oh, you got a bed time?"

"Look, I ain't stayin' up all damn night. What do you want?"

"I just wanna see you." He stepped towards her but she stopped him with a stiff arm.

"It ain't like that no more," she snapped.

"C'mon baby." He reached for her thigh.

"I said, no!" she pushed his hand away. She hoped he wouldn't notice her nipples getting hard.

"Fe-Fe, damn," he protested. "I really been thinkin' about you."

"Nigga please!" she exclaimed. "You need to be missin' the freaks you got in Durham, so don't come at me with that lame game."

"You think I'm runnin' game? Word on my life I wanna get back wit you."

She laughed in his face. "Who you think you foolin'?"

He took a glance and slid closer. "Fe-Fe, I'm the deal real. What I gotta do to prove it? Fuck them freaks in Durham."

"Teck, you come on a booty call and talkin' bout you wanna be with me. All you want is the bomb pussy. You don't give a damn about me."

"Listen baby, believe me. I know I fucked up and let the paper get to my head. But I got on my feet because of you baby. I want to make it like it used to be. You and me, fuck everything else. Let a nigga prove it." He moved his hand to her warm, soft thigh and grinned at the two imprints of her nipples. Fe-Fe looked into his eyes as he slid his hand higher up her thigh. When he moved closer, she moved away from him until her back touched the arm of the couch. She felt his fingers rub against her pussy lips. She opened her legs. Then she changed her mind. "No, Teck, no!" Tammy's death flashed into her mind. In Fe-Fe's heart, she felt like Teck and Wallo had something to do with Tammy's death.

"You fuckin' bitch!"

Chapter 10

"ANSHON, PHONE!" Wood C shouted from the kitchen.

"Speak," Anshon said when Wood C handed him the phone.

"This Anshon?" a soft voice asked.

"Yeah, who dis?"

"This is Larrisha."

"Look, your plan is taking too fuckin' long. You got somethin' or not?"

"Yes. I have a name."

"What is it?"

"Kristi, Kristi Connelly. She's drives a gold Lexus

and her license plate reads UGT411. Her address is 123 Maine Street and her sister's name is Constance Connelly. She's a prison guard. The ball is now in your court."

As Anshon stormed out the door to his Chevy with Deck and Wood C on his heels, he could only think of revenge for his sister.

They stopped in Clayton first, Deck picked up his MAC-11 then the three moved on to Cary. Wood C and Anshon were already strapped. Wood C had two glocks and Anshon had his gorilla back in his lap.

"Stay within the speed limit," Wood C cautioned as Anshon became heavy on the gas. "We don't need to get caught behind no bullshit."

Once they reached Cary, it took them close to thirty minutes to find Kristi's place and just as Larrisha promised, a gold Lexus E330 was sitting in the parking lot.

****

Kristi was in the kitchen talking to her sister, Constance, and making plans to tell Anshon the truth about Wallo and Teck.

Anshon knocked on the door.

"Who is it?" Kristi, asked politely.

"Somebody order pizza?" asked the voice from behind the closed door.

"Let me call you back, Constance." After hanging up the phone, she looked through the peephole to see who she thought was a pizza delivery man with his back turned. *They're always getting the duplex numbers wrong*, she thought. Kristi opened the door and before she could say a word, two masked men forced their way in. Wood C backed up and tossed the empty pizza box he found in the dumpster to the floor, as he pulled his mask down.

Deck went to search the rooms with the MAC-11 as Wood C took up his spot by the window. Anshon had the gorilla pointed at Kristi's head as Deck cased the place to make sure she was alone.

"Now," Anshon said from behind the masked face. "I want some fuckin' answers Kristi Connelly and I want the right ones!" He pointed a black gloved finger at her.

Kristi was cringed up on her sofa with her eyes locked on the big gun stuck in her face. "Now, question number one," Anshon said. "Where do you work?"

"At...a bank," she said trembling.

"Is Constance your sister?"

"Yes," she cried.

"Now tell me what happened when the young lady in the white Mercedes truck was killed."

"I don't recall." She shrugged her shoulders.

Anshon cocked the hammer back making the 5-shot chamber slowly rotate. The loud click made tears fall from her eyes. Kristi buried her face in her hands.

"Bitch! You got Alzheimer's or sumthin'? Now let's try this again." He yanked her up by her hair and placed the 8 1/2 inch barrel to her head.

"Please!" she sobbed. "Oh God, p-please don't kill me."

"Don't kill you? Do you think the woman in the Mercedes truck begged for her life?! Now SHUT UP!" he shouted. "And answer my fuckin' question!" His voice was laced with anger. Kristi slumped to the floor as he shoved her to the ground. "Answer the question!"

"I w-went to work," she cried, "at the b-bank that day."

"And!"

"I…left w-w-work early."

"Go on!"

"I called my baby's Father-"

"Teck?"

"Yes."

"And what?" Anshon said through clinched teeth.

Tears slowly fell from Kristi's eyes as she came clean. "It was Teck and Wallo. Not me…or my sister. I swear to God it wasn't us."

"Bitch if you wanna live you better give me the right answer!" Anshon said with the gun back to her head. "Did dem clowns rob my sister—"

"Yo!" Wood C exclaimed. But it was too late. Anshon had slipped up and gave a clue to who he was.

"Anshon, please," Kristi cried.

"Man, shit!" Deck cursed. They knew what had to be done.

"Please don't kill me," she cried on her knees. "I

187

didn't know they were gonna kill your sister. I was gonna call you anyway...me and my sister."

"Let's go see them niggas!" Wood C said. "Fuck all this talk!"

Anshon took a deep breath to slow his heartbeat down. He glanced at Deck. Deck nodded his head.

"Please don't kill me, Anshon," she pleaded. "Please, oh God," she cried.

He slowly backed up and she ran toward him. "Slow the fuck down!"

Wood C came up from behind, grabbed her chin, and placed a hand on her forehead. Snapping her neck, her body jerked around on the floor for a few seconds before she dropped dead.

A few minutes later, they were back in the Chevy with Wood C behind the wheel. "Which twin we gettin' first?" Wood C asked.

Anshon shrugged his shoulders with tears running down his face. "My sister told me," he sniffed, "that you can take care of your enemies but you need God to help you with your friends...and she ain't never lied."

"Let's do this shit right y'all!" Wood C said. "Let's

lay these clowns down on the low so we can still walk da streets. I ain't goin' to prison and ain't gonna go on the run so let's think this shit through ai'ight?"

"No doubt!" Deck added from the back.

****

Wallo, who was still pretending to be Teck, woke up with a broken glass bottle to his throat. Fe-Fe looked him in the eyes, "I done been on the streets long enough to let a nigga know that I ain't the one. If I say don't fuckin touch me, don't fuckin' touch me."

Wallo, looked at Fe-Fe like she was crazy. "You got that ma, you got that."

The real Teck was in Redwood with Constance. He stood in her kitchen with Wallo's motorcycle helmet in his hand as Constance tried to call her sister Kristi for the third time.

"I don't understand why she's not picking up the phone," Constance said.

"Try your Momma's crib," Teck suggested.

"I know she's not there."

Teck glanced at his watch. "Find that bitch!" he spat. "And you better know where she is by the time I get back!"

Constance just wanted Teck to leave so she and Kristi could carry out the plan to tell Anshon about Teck and Wallo.

"Where you going?" Constance asked.

"Back to the storage to get my ride and park his."

"Why y'all switch?" Constance pressed.

"Does it matter!" he said putting the helmet on. Teck knew his brother was over Fe-Fe's. The original plan was for Teck to kill Constance because she was beginning to talk too much. When she first started fucking with Anshon in prison, the plan was for her to find out where Anshon and Tammy kept their work and their stash; but for some reason Anshon didn't let Constance get to close to him.

Constance figured she'd take a shower before she headed to Cary. She tried calling Kristi but was receiving no answer. Constance stepped out of the shower ten minutes later. She wrapped the towel over her breasts and tip toed into her bedroom. She nearly slipped and fell on her ass when she found Anshon sitting on her bed.

"H-how did you get in here?" she asked. "Better yet...why are you here?"

"The door was opened up when I knocked," he

lied. He had come through the back door by picking the lock after creeping through the woods. "Me and my girl got into a fight.".

"Oh," Constance smiled. "Well, in that case." She took the towel off and walked towards him. She made her breast jiggle from side to side. "So you miss me huh?" she reached for his hand placing it between her legs.

"Wallo ain't gonna show?"

"No baby. He's in High Point." She sat next to him and went to work at his zipper. "Baby, I miss this so much," she purred pulling his dick out and playing with it. He didn't say nothing as she buried her face in his lap and starting sucking his dick...he was kind enough to hold her wet hair. She really got into it, bobbing up and down with quick motions. "Mmmmmmmmmm!" she moaned as she took him deeper into her wet mouth. Making him cum with the last stroke of her tongue.

"Drink that cum baby," he moaned as she lapped it up, "that's it." He stroked her hair. "All of it." Once she was done and lifted her head up to ask if he had a condom so they could fuck, he placed the 8 1/2 barrel of his revolver to her soft pink lips.

"Pretend that this a big black dick. Like the one you

191

just finish sucking on." Slowly he stood up with the gorilla in her face as he fixed his pants. "Where Teck and Wallo?" he asked.

"Huh?"

"Bitch, you know the saying. If you can say huh, you can hear. Yeah, I know all about what you did to my sister!"

Constance slid back towards the headboard shivering. "WHAT ARE YOU TALKING ABOUT!" she screamed.

He tried to quiet her by smacking her upside the head with the 4 1/2 pound. Just his luck, he did it too hard and opened a bleeding gash near her hairline. She was stunned.

"WHERE THEY AT?" he hissed in her ear.

"S-storage," she cried, freigthened by the blood trickling down her face.

"What?"

"S-storage...he's gone to get his van, in Clayton."

"Did the twins kill my sister?"

"Yes," she nodded, the blood was beginning to collect in the corner of her mouth.

"They shot my sister the first time too?" He yanked her hair back.

"Yes," she cried.

Anshon couldn't help the tears falling from his eyes. "Bitch you could've told me about the twins. Then my sister would be alive!" Anshon pulled the trigger back and shot Constance twice in the head as she spent her last breath begging for her life. "And that's on the strength of you Tammy," Anshon mumbled. He spit on Constance's body on his way out. "Dumb bitch!"

Teck was halfway to Clayton when he realized he'd left the keys to the storage in Constance's bedroom. He made a quick u-turn then gunned the engine bringing the front wheel in the air. When the wheel touched the pavement, he was going 91 mph. He reached Redwood in record-breaking time. He left his helmet on as he went up to the door. He knocked. When she didn't answer, he opened the door with his brother's key. Once inside, he called out her name as he slid the tinted visor up. He ran up the stairs and called her name out once again. He opened the bedroom door. "Yo Constance, I forgot-" He paused at the sight before him. "Constance!" he shouted "What the fuck! Constance!"

Constance's blood was flowing from the bed and covered half the floor. Teck pulled off his helmet and fell to his knees, "What the fuck happened!" he shouted. He jumped up and raced out the door. Not knowing where he would end up, he knew he had to get the hell out. He hopped on his bike and before he realized where he was headed he found himself pulling up to Fe-Fe's.

Fe-Fe was still curled up in the bed when her doorbell rung. She jumped up and ran towards the door, praying it was Anshon. She looked at the person standing at her door and saw it was the real Teck. "Oh my God!" she screamed, "Wallo tried to rape me." She fell into Teck's arms, "Teck, can you believe it? He's up stairs!"

Teck pushed her away and started calling for his brother to come down stairs, "Wallo! Wallo!" Wallo jumped up and ran down the stairs. "I know what the plan was," Teck said, "But somebody else killed Constance, it's some shit in the game."

"What!" Wallo screamed.

Teck took a deep breath then explained to his brother how he found Constance. Teck and Wallo were so upset about not knowing what the hell was going on that they didn't pay Fe-Fe any mind as she went to her bedroom. She called Anshon on his cell phone.

She quickly told Anshon that the twins were over and that some crazy shit was going down. Just as she was about to mention Constance, she heard the phone click off. Fe-Fe quickly got dressed and quietly ran back down the stairs. She tipped in the kitchen and grabbed a knife. She wanted to sneak out the back door, but she was scared the twins might hear her and shoot her. So she just laid low with a knife tucked under the hoody she had on.

In the living room she found Wallo sitting in the couch with his face buried in his hands crying as Teck paced the floor with his cell phone to his ear, trying to call Kristi.

Teck was shook. He couldn't reach Kristi. He pushed the redial button for the third time. "Baby, please pick up," he said as he tapped his fist to his lips. After the ninth ring, he hung up. "I'm out. Stay here until I get back," Teck instructed, I'ma go see Kristi."

"Fe-Fe," Teck looked around the room, "don't let him leave. And Wallo," he looked at him, "don't fuck with her." Teck headed for the door.

"Nigga dis ain't Holiday fuckin' Inn!" she snapped.

"Both y'all asses can step!" she pointed towards the front door.

Teck turned around and pointed the black .40 cal at Fe-Fe's chest. "You heard what the fuck I said! Now talk slick and see if I don't make light shine through your body!"

Fe-Fe wasn't stupid. She nodded her head up and down.

When Teck stepped outside, Selma's finest were slowly riding down the street three deep. They saved his life because Anshon, Wood C and Deck were sitting in the cut waiting on his ass. Anshon looked at his boys, "He got a way for now and only now."

Fe-Fe sat on her couch with her arms folded as Wallo sat at the other end crying. When two taps sounded at the door, it flew open before Fe-Fe could answer it. Anshon came in, followed by Wood C and Deck. Wallo figured he was still in the clear. He didn't look up until he heard Fe-Fe say, "Oh shit!"

He looked up to see Anshon standing over him with the biggest revolver he'd ever seen in his life. Fe-Fe stood up but Wood C motioned for her to sit down.

"Why muthafucka?" Anshon sobbed. "What the fuck my sister ever do wrong to your bitch ass?"

Wallo lowered his head.

"ANSWER ME!" Anshon shouted, placing the barrel on Wallo's forehead.

Wallo shrugged his shoulders then placed his hand on the armrest of the couch. Fe-Fe started to scream. Anshon looked at her, "He got a .380 stashed between the seats," she said.

Before Anshon could do anything, Deck punched Wallo in the mouth then picked up the .380. Wood C was at the window with his two heaters. Anshon glanced at Fe-Fe as tears filled her eyes. He didn't have to speak. He nodded his head once.

"Where Teck go?" Anshon asked Wallo.

Wallo's mouth was bleeding badly. He wiped his mouth shrugging his shoulders.

"Nigga, he just left!" Anshon said, then he hit him with the .50 up side his head before he told another lie.

"F-fuck you. Ain't givin' up my brother," Teck said.

"MY SISTER DEAD 'CAUSE OF YOUR ASS!" Anshon screamed.

After that was said, he handed his revolver to Deck

then started to pound Wallo with hard blows to the face and body. Fe-Fe wanted to feel sorry for Wallo, but she couldn't, after all, he tried to rape her and he killed Tammy. When Deck told Anshon to ease up, Wallo was left on the floor with his face badly bruised up. Fe-Fe started to cry as Anshon took her to the back room after she told them where Teck was headed. When he closed Fe-Fe's bedroom door behind him, she broke down and asked him not to kill her.

"What?" he asked her surprised. "I love you. I'm in love with you. Why would I kill you?

Fe-Fe didn't know what to say, so she fell into his arms. "I know we can't be together so I've been trying to fight this shit. But it gets harder everyday." Fe-Fe's mouth dropped open. "Anshon...I-I—I'm pregnant."

"Damn, baby." Anshon rubbed her face.

"Don't worry now." She assured him, "Please don't."

"Okay, okay," he said trying to shake what Fe-Fe had just told him.

"The twins killed Tammy, Fe-Fe. You know I gotta do what I gotta do."

Fe-Fe hugged him. "I'm on your side Anshon, always know that." She stood on her toes and kissed him on the forehead before he left. She caught him by his shirt as he was turning to leave. "I love you."

He winked his eye at her and ran back down the stairs. Fe-Fe prayed that she would see him again.

****

Teck made it back to Selma two hours later. Because he was in a panic and speeding, he'd led a five highway state patrols on a high-speed chase until he lost them on a back road in Wilson Mills. He didn't care because he was still in shock after finding Kristi's body at her duplex. Kristi wasn't suppose to die. That was the deal he and Wallo had. It was suppose to only be Constance. *What the fuck is going on?* Teck thought.

Teck felt pain and hate at the same time. He pulled up in Fe-Fe's driveway and found a note on the front door. He instantly recognized his brother's handwriting and didn't try to reason why his brother wanted him to go to the school bus parking lot at Triple S. He took the back roads and hit Buffalo Road.

When he reached the parking lot, he spotted his brother's forest green Nissan Quest parked in front of the gym with its lights off. When he neared the Nisson Quest, he noticed the driver side window was down and with a closer inspection, he saw his brother slumped over the wheel. He brought his motorcycle to a screeching halt and jumped off. Teck was reaching for the Quest's door handle when suddenly the side door slid back.

"Yeah nigga!" Deck said pointing the MAC-11 at Teck's chest. When Teck looked at who he thought was his brother, he saw Wood C, grinning at him, gold fronts and all. "See you in hell pot'nah!"

Teck turned slowly to see Anshon stepping from behind the minivan holding the golden .50 cal pointed at his head. Teck wasn't as brave as his brother. He threw his hands up in defeat. Wood C stepped out and relieved Teck of his .40. Teck had never felt so much fear in his life as Wood C yanked his helmet off.

"LOOK AT ME!" Anshon shouted.

Teck slowly turned his head towards Anshon as the gold 8 1/2 inch barrel touched his forehead.

"You was my ma'fuckin' pot'nah niggah. We stole on niggahs together and this is the shit that you do?" Anshon spat on him. "I remember when I came home from prison, I told you that if I caught the muthafuckers that fucked wit my sis-" Anshon's hand was trembling. Flashes of Tammy's casket being lowered into the ground kept playing in his mind. Then he thought of his niece and nephew growing up without her. "Motherfucker!" Before pulling the trigger he wanted to ask Teck why, but deep down he didn't want to know.

Wood C took a step back as Anshon wiped his eyes. Deck did the same. Wood C happened to glance towards the road to see two sets of headlights coming. "Yo, Shon wait."

BOOM. Too late.

As the State Troppers cars drove nearer, they heard the echoing sound from the blast and the flash from the barrel was bright and distinctive. Instantly, the lead State Trooper hit the blue lights and the gas.

Wood C took off running towards the lunchroom. Deck stepped in front of the minivan and made the MAC-11 speak. Anshon ran towards the gym and fired a shot at the lock. Deck was on his heels two seconds later. They could hear the two State Troopers sliding to a halt as they busted through the double doors, looking for their suspects. Wood C had crept his way to the student parking lot and was still moving. He headed for the woods to hopefully disappear before the back-up K-9 unit came. Wood C loved his freedom. Fuck prison. Anshon and Deck were just running past the front office when the two State Troopers let off with their glock 9mm. Deck slid to the floor and rolled to his right as Anshon dove to the left. They could both hear the State Troopers calling for backup. Deck stuck the MAC-11 around the corner and squeezed off eight shots. The barrage sent the State Troopers for cover. Deck got up and took off running while changing the empty 32-round clip. As Deck ran for the lunchroom, Anshon made his move. It was hard to fire on the run with the .50, its kick back was too big for a one-hand shot. He was breathing heavily as he took off towards the library. It was better to split up. He knew he would never see the free world if he was caught. He quickly reloaded the two empty shots in his .50 with shaky hands. "Fuck!" he whispered at the sounds of police sirens in the distance. He lowered himself to his stomach and moved quickly behind a row of books in the pitch black library. When he heard the chatter of the police radio near the door, he stopped breathing in hopes they hadn't seen him enter the library. Niggas get a sixth sense when they on the run.

"POLICE!" a deep commanding voice shouted. "COME OUT WITH YOUR HANDS UP!"

Anshon closed his eyes and murmured a quick prayer. But why would God listen to a sinner, he was the bad guy.

"Last warning!" the state trooper stated.

Anshon gripped the gold .50 and kissed the barrel. He made up his mind to save one round....he refused to live and die in prison.

"You and me baby girl," he whispered hyping himself up. He slowly came up on one knee and peeked between some books. He only saw one of the State Troopers as he ducked behind the checkout counter; gun in hand. His heart was pounding in his ears. He searched for the second State Trooper, but came up short. He slowly slid a thick hardcover book from the shelf. The police sirens were still in the distance. He had to get ghost before the backup showed up. He gripped the book, slung it clear across the library, and was moving in the opposite direction before it struck the computer room door. The hidden State Trooper made his presence known by squeezing off two loud shots in the area where he saw the book thrown from. Anshon dove to the floor. These muthafuckas wasn't playing any more. He cocked back the hammer and turned just in time to catch the State Trooper in the moonlight as he moved from behind the checkout counter.

Anshon brought up the gorilla with a firm two-hand grip while on one knee. He knew he had to go all out. He eased back on the trigger, BOOM! Then he rolled to his left. The hidden State Trooper who was calling his partner over saw how the impact of the gun lifted him off his feet completely and flipped back over the checkout counter. The .50 packed so much power that it took the State Trooper's entire right arm off.

Anshon heard the hidden State Trooper gasp in shock near the reading lounge. BOOM! BOOM! BOOM! Glass shattered from the buzzing slugs from the .50. He took off for the door while he had the chance. Just as he excited the library, the police back-up slid into the student drop off loop six deep. He took off towards the lunchroom.

"OFFICER DOWN!" he heard someone scream behind him. "DOWN THE HALL, FREEZE!"

By instinct, he dove to the glossy floor sliding on his stomach as the deadly line of lead ripped down the hall. They kept firing down the dark hallway trying to pin Anshon down. Anshon could see blue lights out in the student parking lot. They were trying to trap him off. They were still firing as he rolled towards the hall-way leading to the brick masonry class. Once in the hallway, he stumbled to his feet and took off running full speed. He had to hit the back exit and try to get ghost in the woods. He was on pure adrenalin as he reached the fire exit. The alarm blared once he burst through the fire exit. A sheriff's deputy patrol car was slowing to a stop just as his feet touched the pave-ment. BOOM! The entire front windshield exploded.

The rookie deputy was leaning over and looked up where the headrest used to be. He shifted in reverse without ever looking up. He planned to resign tomorrow.

Anshon ran between two outside trailer-like classrooms and quickly reloaded the five empty slots. Taking four quick breaths, he dashed across the band practice field and headed for the woods. The police were done with a verbal warning. The trooper that Anshon had shot in the library was dead.

Anshon had reached the woods then he tripped over a log. When he struggled to his feet, he turned to see countless moving flashlights and in the center was the barking K-9. He turned and bent down over the long barrel. He didn't know if his shot would reach, but he'd let'em know what would be waiting.

Back at the fire exit, the K-9 officer was about to let his dog go when suddenly a deputy standing five feet from him holding a pump was thrown back on his ass followed by the report from Anshon's .50 BOOM! They all scattered. They couldn't return any fire because there were houses not far from the woods. The slug had reached out and touched the deputy in the upper chest. It didn't punch through the vest, but the slug packed enough stopping power to make the deputy's heart stop.

Anshon was already on the run when the deputy hit the ground. He ran a good distance until he found the running trail used by the track and field team. He stopped and crouched to the ground. He could see them searching the woods to his left. He placed the .50 on the ground and quickly took his Nikes off. He removed both socks then found two rocks. He had to trick that fucking K-9 if he wanted to stand any chance of getting away. He wiped both socks under his arms and vigorously wiped his ass with them. He then placed a rock in each sock and quickly pissed on both. The time to complete his deception took 48 seconds. He slung one to the left and then slung the other to the right then took off running with the gold .50 at a measured pace. He'd run for 30 to 40 seconds then stop and listen. He repeated this until he circled out of the woods near the football practice field. He could see countless squad cars in the bus parking lot.

Teck's minivan was parked in the same spot and when a police car pulled off, he saw the lights shining on the nearly headless Teck, who'd been killed and pushed under his mini-van earlier. Anshon watched and caught his breath. Just because it was dark, he knew it didn't mean he was safe or well hidden. Two minutes later, he made his move to cross the road. Once he made it safely across the street, he ran through the field. Once he reached the woods, he knew he'd be straight. He reached the thick woods and ran through a brier patch. The thorns hooked him in a thousand spots, but it would take more than some thorns to stop him from running from the police. Since he still had on the gloves, he pulled the briers loose and surged deeper into the woods. When he reached a cow field, he slowed up. He took the time to catch his breath once again and loaded the one empty chamber leaving him with four slugs in his pocket and five in the golden chamber. He nearly shitted on himself when his cell phone rung. "Shit!" he lowered himself closer to the ground and silenced the ringer.

"Yeah, who dis," he said, licking his dry lips.

"Wood C, nigga, where you at?" Wood C whispered.

"N-near a cow field," Anshon replied then shot the same question back to Wood C.

"Hiding in somebody's back yard under a truck," Wood C whispered. "Deck ain't answering his phone, you seen 'im?"

"We split up at the school," Anshon whispered while looking around with quick jerks.

"Yo…I'ma holla."

"Ai'ight."

When he slid the slim phone back into his chest pocket, he went back on the move. The cows ignored him as he crouched down near the fence. He thought of his sister as he stood up to jog across another field. The pain was still there. His quest for revenge hadn't changed a damn thing, except his fate. Tammy's words of advice rang in his mind, "Don't let the game be your demise..." Anshon prayed to God to let him reach Peedin Street. If not, he'd be beggin' for the Lord to let him in Heaven's door. So he kept running. He knew he had to be careful crossing Highway 70, so he paused at the edge of the woods and waited for the right chance. Anshon realized the spot he was in was spelling out his life to him. He could see the overpass and further down 70 to his left was a place he never wanted to see again, prison. To his right and a few miles down the road was the cemetery, a place where his sister and Momma rested in peace, a place he wasn't ready to visit just yet, but if it came down to it, he'd pick the right over the left. That left nothing but moving forward to reach home. He said Monica's name, laced up his kicks, cocked the hammer back and dashed across the four-lane highway. His inspection didn't pick out the two Selma's finest parked in the cut.

"FREEZE, POLICE!"

Chapter 11

Monica sat at her kitchen table next to Fe-Fe with her hand on her cell phone and the cordless on the table. The two women were both worried about the same man. When Fe-Fe told Monica about the twins, she nearly fainted. There was no doubt in her mind that Anshon would kill them both. She just wanted her man to come home. Fuck everything else.

"You sure they didn't tell you where they took Wallo?" Monica asked with tears running down her face.

Fe-Fe shook her head slowly side to side. They both had their car keys within reach and when Monica's cordless phone rung she answered it before the first ring was completed. "Hello!" she prayed she would hear Anshon's voice. It was Deck. He told her that he needed a ride and that he would meet her at the Pizza Hut in Smithfield. Deck had put some miles on his Reeboks and was in the clear. He had ditched his MAC-11. When he told her that Wood C and Anshon was still on the run, she nearly dropped the phone. Fe-Fe rushed to pick it up and Deck repeated everything he'd just said to Monica. Fe-Fe snatched up her keys and ran out the door to go pick up the stranded Deck. Monica sat back down and started to cry uncontrollably. She wanted Anshon.

****

Wood C had somehow made it to McDonald's on 301 and was now sitting in the front eating his meal and trying to blend in. Police were still heading down towards the high school. He'd broke his cellphone when he dove from a pair of headlights as he crept through the white neighborhood next to the school's campus. Once he was in the clear he dropped his two .40's in a plastic trashcan. He planned to calm his nerves down then bum a ride back to Selma, which he guessed would be easy. He was biting into his Quarter Pounder when he saw Fe-Fe's Legend slow down for a red light on 301.

Fe-Fe was still praying for Anshon as she sat at the red light. It was a long wait and just as she came off the brake, Wood C swung the door open scaring the shit out of Fe-Fe.

"Go, go, go, go, go, go, go, go, go, go!" Wood C said slamming the door. She pulled off. They both tried to talk at the same time. Fe-Fe won. She told him about Deck then asked about Anshon. Wood C was happy to hear about Deck, but as of now, Anshon was still on the run. "Once we pick up Deck, hit Buffalo Road. Lemme see your cell phone." He checked the side mirror, no blue lights. Fe-Fe told him she didn't have a cell phone. "Damn!" he said slamming his fist on the dashboard. Deck was standing in the parking lot when they pulled up. When he saw Wood C, he asked about Anshon as he got into the backseat. Deck pulled out his phone and quickly dialed Anshon's cell number, he didn't answer.

"Roadblock." Fe-Fe sighed as they rounded the corner near Smithfield Middle School. Blue lights were everywhere.

"FUCK!" Wood C said. When a helicopter flew over with a blinding spotlight, Wood C clenched his fist. The police had Buffalo Road locked down and made them turn around.

Anshon was on the run again, and this time they were on his ass. He had followed their command to freeze, but a passing 18-wheeler had blinded the four police that were two deep in each squad car. Anshon made the .50 throw up. He eased back on the trigger making the gorilla erupt in his hand. Boom! A slug punched a police in the chest killing him instantly. Boom! A slug flattened a tire. Boom! A slug shattered the second squad car's side window. He took off for the woods and reloaded the .50 on the run. Five shots left. God had to be looking down on him when he tripped over a tree stump, as the police opened up with an AR-15 talking in rapid succession. Branches fell on his back as the rapid fire continued to blaze over his head. He fired one shot over his shoulders. Boom! When the helicopter roared over the treetops with it's bright light, he became disoriented. He got himself together, came to his feet, and ran. Fuck looking back, he wanted to move forward. Thorns cut into his face and neck tearing at his skin, but he kept moving without missing a step. Pain would come later. His chest was on fire, but he kept running. When he ran into the dog pound he knew he was almost home. He was about to cut the right when something hot hit him in the arm spinning him around. He slammed into a tree. He rolled over to his stomach and easily found the gleaming .50. His left arm had been hit by a stray round. Ignoring his useless arm, he got up and ran. He could hear the police yelling out to each other as the helicopter buzzed the treetops with it's blinding light. He dove to the ground just as the spotlight moved over him. He gritted his teeth and willed his wounded arm to support the .50. He raised it up as the spotlight moved near him. When the light blinded him, he eased back on the trigger. BOOM! He completely missed the light, but the slang easily punched through the bottom-viewing window in the cockpit and hit the co-pilot in the stomach after the slug first traveled up through his leg. The pilot shrieked and banked the helicopter in a tight turn as the co-pilot spewed blood all over the cockpit. Taking a deep breath, he got up and ran through the woods. Anshon burst out of the woods running as fast as could. His heart was pounding, sweat covered his face, which set his face on fire from the open cuts. He ran in the angle that would allow him to go through his backyard. He could see Selma's finest accelerating down Peedin Street five deep with the blue lights flashing. Suddenly, Anshon stumbled and fell flat on his face.

Monica ran to the front door when the police rode by. Deck had called to tell her than Anshon was still on the run. Tears ran down her face as she looked down the road. Plum and Dee were also standing outside. "Baby, Please." Monica cried to herself. "Please come home."

213

****

Deck was on his way back to Peedin Street with Fe-Fe. Wood C was now sitting behind a bush at the corner of Preston and Massey Street when he saw the K-9 unit coming. Just as it reached his hiding spot, he ran to the curb and emptied Deck's little .32. POP, POP, POP, POP, POP, POP. It caused the driver to lose control and hit the curb at 40mph breaking the rim as the tire blew. Wood C hoped it would help. He took off running and vanished with ease.

****

Anshon was almost home, but he was past exhausted. He was now in the field behind his trailer. His cell phone didn't work so he had to make a quiet entrance. He was bleeding badly, but the wound could have been worse. He fell to his knees then rolled to his side. He was too tired, too weak. He silently cried. He got up once more, but collapsed after five steps. As he was getting to his feet, he heard the K-9 and knew it would follow his blood trail and if the dog didn't kill him, the police would. He came up to his knees as he heard the K-9 rushing through the woods. He refused to go back to prison. "Big Sis!" he sobbed as he held the .50 to his head. He closed his eyes and slowly eased back on the trigger...

EPILOGUE

Ten Months Later, May 2005
Selma, NC

Fe-Fe stood at the gravesite holding her two month old baby girl, Tammy, with grief resting in her heart. Next to her stood Monica holding her six-week-old baby boy, Anshon. And she too had grief resting in her heart. They were both paying their respects for someone they cared about deeply and missed. Monica placed a single red rose on the gravesite as tears rolled down her cheek. After they said their silent goodbyes, they both turned to hug each other.

"You be safe, okay," Fe-Fe said.

Monica wiped her eyes. "I will, Fe-Fe. Just stay in touch with me."

215

"I promise," Fe-Fe said before she turned to leave.

Monica watched her best friend slowly walk away. She was happy for Fe-Fe and Wood C, who were now together. Fe-Fe had legal custody of her twins again and the five of them lived up in Richmond, VA…really it was six if you wanted to count the new seed Wood C had baking in Fe-Fe's oven. Fe-Fe hated lying to Monica about Wood C being lil' Tammy's father. But little did Fe-Fe know, Monica knew the truth, the baby looked too much like Anshon for anything to be denied.

As Wood C neared his gleaming 300C, he opened the door for his queen then kissed her lightly on the lips. They both waved goodbye then slowly pulled out of the quiet cemetery, and that was Fe-Fe's and Wood C's ending.

As for Deck, he was still in Selma. He now runs a barbershop on Raiford that supported his brand new triple wide trailer out in Southern Estates. He no longer took up space in Wood C's 300C passenger seat…he now had Anshon's Chevy.

Larrisha and her brother, Von moved to Los Angeles.

Monica neared the shiny QX56 then wiped her teary eyes. She leaned over to kiss her baby. A few moments later, they were heading for I-95 south to begin a new life down in Miami, Florida. Tammy made her promise her before she died that they would take spot the in Miami, as soon as Anshon got out the game. "Well baby," Monica looked up to the sky, "I guess this is it."

ORDER FORM

Triple Crown Publications
2959 Stelzer Rd.
Columbus, Oh 43219

Name: _____

Address: _____

City/State: _____

Zip: _____

		TITLES	PRICES
		Dime Piece	$15.00
		Gangsta	$15.00
		Let That Be The Reason	$15.00
		A Hustler's Wife	$15.00
		The Game	$15.00
		Black	$15.00
		Dollar Bill	$15.00
		A Project Chick	$15.00
		Road Dawgz	$15.00
		Blinded	$15.00
		Diva	$15.00
		Sheisty	$15.00
		Grimey	$15.00
		Me & My Boyfriend	$15.00
		Larceny	$15.00
		Rage Times Fury	$15.00
		A Hood Legend	$15.00
		Flipside of The Game	$15.00
		Menage's Way	$15.00

SHIPPING/HANDLING (Via U.S. Media Mail)   **$3.95**

TOTAL $_____

FORMS OF ACCEPTED PAYMENTS:

Postage Stamps, Institutional Checks & Money Orders, all mail in orders take 5-7 Business days to be delivered.

ORDER FORM

Triple Crown Publications
2959 Stelzer Rd.
Columbus, Oh 43219

Name: _____

Address: _____

City/State: _____

Zip: _____

		TITLES	PRICES
		Still Sheisty	$15.00
		Chyna Black	$15.00
		Game Over	$15.00
		Cash Money	$15.00
		Crack Head	$15.00
		For the Strength of You	$15.00
		Down Chick	$15.00
		Dirty South	$15.00
		Cream	$15.00
		Hood Winked	$15.00
		Bitch	$15.00
		Stacy	$15.00
		Life Without Hope	$15.00

SHIPPING/HANDLING (Via U.S. Media Mail) $3.95

TOTAL $_____

FORMS OF ACCEPTED PAYMENTS:
Postage Stamps, Institutional Checks & Money Orders, all mail in orders take 5-7 Business days to be delivered.